ISSUE ONE

EDITED BY

LH MAYNARD & MPN SIMS
AND
DAVID J HOWE

One

Published by
ENIGMATIC PRESS &
BFS PUBLICATIONS
2000

Porcelain © 2000 Derek M. Fox
Remember Me Yesterday (first published in Icarus Descending) © 1999 Steve Savile
The Destroyers © 2000 Paul Finch
The Winter Hunt © 2000 Steve Lockley & Paul Lewis
Curves and Sharp Edges © 2000 Tim Lebbon
Introduction © 2000 Maynard & Sims

This collection © 2000 LH Maynard, MPN Sims and David J Howe
Artwork © 2000 Bob Covington and David Bezzina

ISBN 0-9537476-5-4 (paperback)

Publishers contact address
3 Tamworth Close, Reading, Berkshire, RG6 4EQ

Printed by
TTA Press. 5 Martins Lane, Witcham,
Ely, Cambs, CB6 2LB, England

CONTENTS

ILLUSTRATIONS

INTRODUCTION

Some measure life by experience, and welcome each new adventure as a blessing bestowed upon them to enrich their existence. If you think like that then the stories you are about to read will enhance your literary horizons and give pleasure possibly in a way you may not have experienced before.

If you would rather read just Fantasy then there is plenty here to please you, and in pleasing it will be with purity of spirit and quality of technique. If you prefer the supernatural tale there are stories included in the contents that will give tingle to the most jaded of palates, and produce shivers even on the warmest of days.

This book is a unique experience in that it contains a mixture of the supernatural, and the fantastic. It blends both genres effortlessly and successfully with five stories that come from the best writers around in the UK.

Derek M Fox gives us an enigmatic beginning that suggests and whispers in a seemingly classical way until we are enticed and beguiled. Steve Savile deals fluently and with poetic prose about something that might be happening, but which leads to a chilling conclusion nevertheless. Paul Finch gives us a historically based yarn almost epic in its telling, with the fantasies and details merging magnificently. Steve Lockley and Paul Lewis provide a modern fantasy that has its roots in a time far from modern. Tim Lebbon lets his imagination run in rainbow patterns as his own world of fantasy brings our selection to a close.

Add to that the superior artwork of Bob Covington and David Bezzina, and we hope you enjoy the experience.

It has been a new experience for both The British Fantasy Society and Enigmatic Press, but we think it has worked well. And now, reader, it's over to you…

Maynard & Sims / David J Howe
September 2000.

F20

PORCELAIN

Derek M. Fox

THE HOUSE BLEEDS.

Sunset lit, Shire House takes on the rich, dark colour of blood – the life force, the very same that kept Claire alive, pumped from my veins into hers by Doctor Schiller.

And most accept that when life ends we die. A pertinent and questionable premise.

The illusion forces me to consider if bricks and stone contain a similar fluid for the simple reason that whenever I survey the three storey grey stone and brick, its dark, secretive windows and its shining black door with brass furniture, I feel it's trying to tell me something, warn me in some way. And the most unnerving aspect. Shire House bleeds all the time, whatever the weather.

Perhaps then the property has a life all its own, especially since Eloise left me some eighteen months ago. And now Claire, the blood having congealed in her young veins. All I have is her legacy: the dolls on the chest outside her room.

Seven months is a long time to be deprived of a second loved one. Some may argue so I say to them: Consider the varying degrees of love, the depth to which one individual feels for another. It can and does go very deep. Others remain cynical – Schiller is one, for his mind is but a shallow swamp stinking with contempt for me and mine.

In times of stress it is easy to remember things we would normally consider insignificant but when Schiller attended Claire that last time I remember everything.

At six eighteen precisely on that stubbornly cool August day in 1899, I summoned Samuel, my groom and general handyman, who hadn't yet gone to the local inn, a habit he'd nurtured over years especially following a hard day's work. I asked him to make haste and fetch the good doctor, Wilhelm

Schiller, a German educated at Leipzig who had taken up residence as GP in our town. Hardly relevant information except to acquaint you with a little of his character, to inform you that this same man also attended my dear wife, Eloise.

Sam, still dressed in his grubby leather jerkin and dark, soil stained trousers, never commented, yet I beheld my own desperation mirrored in his chestnut dark eyes. Urging him to take one of my best horses, a bay of over sixteen hands, I watched from the window of Claire's room as he galloped down the drive, whorls of dust dispersed like the dreams and prayers I'd ever uttered for my sweet child. And my wife.

Desperation underscored a need to see Claire happy, that pink rosy hue embellishing her cheeks; her warm smile as she would pick flowers from the garden, bright eyes wide as I named every plant and shrub she pointed out. Like Eloise, the illness rampaged, tortured Claire's twelve year old frailty, leaving her semi-comatose, her colour matching the pristine white of the pillow upon which she lay.

Strange how a sick room stains Shire House. Any house for that matter. Memories, first of Eloise's dark, pained eyes staring into nothing as her last breath whispered into a sun-kissed day. Of watching Claire succumb to the same wasting disease. Dear God! it is too harrowing for man to bear, seeing loved ones plucked away, seeds scattered in the ether. My one consolation is my belief in the depths to which love can go.

The fetor lingers, the room less bright despite floral bouquets, its throat clogging odour of medicines, of bodily excretions from patients who can no longer attend to common, everyday ablutions.

Claire's room had become entrenched with her stale breathing, and the awful yet evident need to relieve herself. Despite the fact that I kept her washed and always, always dressed in the finest sleeping attire, the aroma cultivated its own putridity with each passing day.

God bless her, not her fault. And I must do everything I could for her, thoughts of her dying difficult to contemplate.

Schiller once advised: 'Never give in to your feelings, Herr Leverton. She has life, you will give her the strength she needs.' The sentiment lacked depth and I scarcely dare accept that he meant it. To me it is the eyes that speak, and when eyes resemble a lake's opaque surface, then any true sentiment remains as drowned as the soul behind them.

The smell grew worse. Claire deteriorated despite a third transfusion from me which left me weak until I partook of sustenance – a chore in itself considering the burden I carried.

No! An ill choice for Claire could never be a burden. She was life itself to me, the only thing I had left, the one who had kept me sane after Eloise...

Forgive my lapses, for it is hard to dwell on some things.

Caring mattered and Claire had my sole attention. My love for her mother, hers for me, I still saw in photographs. What had Schiller done to help her? Surely he must realise that to lose Claire to the same disease...!

Sadly, I did not know that it would be too late to save Claire, or that I would come to despise Schiller's name.

As doctors come, the man had always been attentive, a listening man with a cordial bedside manner. He would joke with patients, especially children. With them he would pretend that the instruments pulled from his grim looking black bag were toys – the spatula for the tongue, the stethoscope which he would breathe on to 'Warm it up' before placing it on their delicate skin. The hypodermic needle he would liken to the nip of a puppy dog's teeth. 'See, so little blood, so not as bad as puppy, ja?'

The children would smile, every neighbour who was a parent confirming this. Claire never did. During one of her lucid moments – admittedly few during those last weeks – she did say: 'Daddy, I don't like Doctor Schiller, he frightens me.'

'Why, sweetheart?' I blamed the fever, thinking her unaware of what she said. I stroked her brow, bathed it with a cool, damp cloth.

'The way he looks at me.'

Something should have warned me but I paid little heed. 'How does he look at you? Like me?'

'Daddy, no! He...he looks at me like I'm no longer here.'

A vague recollection, something Eloise said. I argued against it, believing Schiller's cordial manner could never be deceptive.

'I'm sorry, darling, I don't understand.' I felt jittery inside, like I was entering a dark room very unfamiliar with the premises in which it is housed.

'Please, Claire,' I pressed. 'Explain.'

Her eyes found mine, and I knew, knew instantly that she spoke the truth, not that she had ever lied. And hadn't I seen the exact opposite of true feeling in Schiller's almost blank eyes?

I shivered and rose from the bed to close the window, hoping to disguise my unease, keep it from my only daughter whose mother had been prematurely taken from us.

Eloise. She and I would joke about all the children we would have, yet she only gave birth to this treasure. We tried but Schiller informed us quite casually one day that it would be impossible, that Eloise could no longer bear children. Perhaps it's the reason why Claire innocently started her collection of dolls, I don't know.

'Daddy,' Claire called, her voice quavering yet quite robust despite her illness, 'you do believe me, don't you?'

What could I say? Truth came as the best option and I nodded to allay her fears. I also promised to remain whenever Schiller examined her, to refuse to be ordered out as he insisted. The unforgettable phrase, his phrase 'A doctor and his patient have no need of help' is now most disagreeable.

Promises are rendered as chaff in the wind because of Schiller's strength of will, his way of insisting, his very attitude when out of earshot of patients, commanding and demanding.

From the window I could see the dark frock coat, the hat jauntily tilted on his head as he dismounted. Samuel held his horse as he unstrapped a huge bag from the saddle. A heavy tread on the stairs, then the landing, muffled by the carpet runner. The pause as he removed his hat to leave it on the chest outside Claire's room. Claire's dolls watch him, yet say nothing.

The dolls: a child's whim, then a habit. 'By having them there,' she told me, 'I can select one each morning before breakfast.' Seven dolls – one for each day of the week.

On that day, I gave Claire her final blood transfusion, Schiller officiating in that austere, cold way he'd adopted when fully aware my daughter hadn't long to live, not that he ever said outright. The transfusion was his way of placating me, keeping me appeased because he knew my depth of feeling.

She rallied shortly after, the pink suffusing her cheeks. Even her eyes shone when she asked: 'Daddy, what day is it?'

I sat on the bed, brushed back blonde hair from her forehead, took her frail hand in mine: it felt like a giant holding a fairy's hand. 'It's Saturday, my sweet.'

'Then I can take my Sunday dolly to church tomorrow.'

I smiled, my heart bubbled with joy. How much it meant to again see and hear her, so sane, so absolutely Claire.

She died at four minutes to midnight ere Sunday had time to breathe.

The following day I buried her beside Eloise in the family plot close to the summerhouse.

We were three, Samuel, and myself, with Schiller standing courteously a few yards distant, his face a nondescript mask. I remember glancing at Eloise's resting place, tears for her mingled with those I wept for Claire.

I placed the Sunday doll on top of Claire's coffin before Samuel filled in the grave. I did not, nor could I, know what Schiller had done. What he knew. Not then. But Samuel, I would learn, thought he knew. As the saying goes: There are none so blind as those who may see.

Seven months ago exactly and I still contemplate the space on the chest, the vague outline of the Sunday doll where it rested against the grey-white wall.

PORCELAIN

As for Schiller, he would call at every pretext despite my insisting he had no patient. However, his penchant for the grape, and his commanding presence forced me to comply.

'After all,' he kept reminding me, 'I cared for your daughter, and so owe it to her father to watch over my patients, alive or dead.'

'What exactly do you mean, Schiller?' I asked the night we sat in my study. He'd beaten me four games to three at draughts, the click of the hard discs on the board matched by the click of his teeth as I crowned yet another of his kings.

The eyes stared – it's in the eyes, I told myself meeting the stare in an oblique, drowsy way. Wine, surely, and the warmth. I never questioned that it could easily be something else.

Suffice to say, I heard only his voice, and glimpsed shimmering firelight from the corner of my eye.

'What do I mean, Robert Leverton? I'll tell you. Believe in life hereafter, that the dead shall rise and once more court the living. Remember, my friend, you gave her your blood. Living blood.'

I sensed rather than saw him rise to leave, passing between myself and the fire, the oil lamp's glow from the desk eclipsed, brightening only when the shadow moved away. At least I think it was Schiller for the door closed, the latch clicked yet in his wake a rankness... of urine and faeces, of vomit, and something more, the sickly aroma of blood.

What happened that evening I cannot guess. Did Schiller exude some power? I remember coming sharply awake in the chair though not in my study, rather in the one I used whenever I sat with Claire. Had I walked here without thinking, bereft of my senses, drunk, what?

September moonlight ranged defiantly across the floor to anoint the bed, the pillow, the depression in it. I muttered a prayer for her soul alerted suddenly to a confusing murmur she would emit if restless.

'Claire?' Nothing. From the stable, two horses whinnied, the sound daunting in the absolute quiet, blending with, rather than detracting from other noises barely above an audible pitch. Tired, blaming excess alongside stupidity over my loss, I stood by the bed.

Slowly, out of respect I caressed her pillow, overwhelmed by the queerest feeling. At the window I studied my right hand, the moonlight collecting several golden hairs.

'Oh great Father in Heaven.' I fell to my knees. Schiller's words taunted: 'You gave her your blood. Living blood.'

I dare not think beyond reality, for to do so might drive me mad. The hairs were from her head, but they would be. I chastised myself for the lapse.

Damn it, this was her bed, her pillow, the slip unchanged since the day she died.

A little afraid to remain there, I staggered onto the landing, it, the stairs and hallway gilded early morning silver. The hairs fluttered from my palm as I caught the chest with my knee hearing a brush of material against the wall as the dolls slid, some tumbling onto the floor, others left askance on the chest. I collected them, having the presence of mind to check each beatific porcelain face for damage. 'Claire, oh my sweet daughter, I'm so sorry.'

Replacing them as best I could in strictest order, I leaned on the banister rail and started to count them. Five? FIVE! 'There should be SIX! The Sunday doll's in the grave! So where–?'

My words stung the empty silence. I counted again, checked the floor. The Saturday doll had disappeared.

In the morning, seated at the table in the huge kitchen, my toast tasting like burlap, I asked Samuel about the doll. He looked pained for always whenever I questioned him, he wore this hangdog look certain I might be about to accuse him of something he hadn't done.

He stood cap in hand, dark hair unruly, his whiskered face resembling that of a naughty puppy. 'I hasn't touched nothin' of Mizz Claire's, soir,' he said in a broad Irish accent that smacked of peat and Guinness-flavoured bars. 'Wouldna dream o' doin' such a ting not with 'er hardly cold, an' then never would I. Respect is what, Mr. Robert, soir, you bein' her father an' all.'

I apologised, and brushed away the accusation. 'Enough then. Go about your business.'

He shuffled his feet, twisted the cap, and without leave pulled out the chair opposite me and sat down. He leaned across, dark gaze holding my questioning one. 'Soir, 'scuse me, an' beggin' your pardon, but there's somethin' I havta say.'

My heart sank. 'Not thinking of leaving are you? Please don't take umbrage at what I said.'

'No Mr. Robert, nothin' o' the sort.'

His twisting the cap annoyed me. I snatched it off him and placed it on the table. 'Now, Sam, out with it, then we can attend to business.'

'Aye, well 'tis like this, Mr. Robert –' He fell silent, eyes everywhere but on me.

'Sam!'

'Sorry.' He looked humbled. 'Somethin' 'bout that last day, 'bout that doctor feller, an'...' He paused. 'P'raps better not, eh?' He made to rise, to grab his cap.

I grabbed it first. 'Sam, don't propose to tell me something and then leave it. You know my moods by now, scarcely helped by – well, you know what I mean. Just say what you have to.'

'It's Schiller killed Mizz Claire,' he blurted. 'As sure as I believe in leprechauns so 'e did.'

I shivered, asked him to close the window which he did. The chill persisted. In my mind I heard Claire telling me she didn't like Schiller. 'Treats me like I'm no longer here.'

'What are telling me, Sam?' I had to know if only to confirm certain suspicions I'd fostered since Eloise died.

''Tis this, Mr. Robert. I was cleanin' windows and watched him from the ladder. He didn't know I was there, an' you always left the room after them transfusion tings. I seen him drain some of the blood back out –'

'HE WHAT?' My chair tipped back, the butter pot teetered on the table's edge, Sam caught it before it fell. Anger sutured my mind. 'Sam, you're telling me that Schiller stole my daughter's blood? Stole my blood?'

A look told me he felt justified. 'I am. Think me an idjit over certain things, but I knows what I sees, an' that there doctor man took the blood that was pumped. He put the bottle in his bag.'

My mind filled with Eloise, her emaciated state, of Schiller attending her as he had Claire. 'What is he trying to do, Sam?' I reared against the sink. 'Am I to be next?' I looked beyond Sam and swore the wall beyond the rack of copper saucepans ran red.

A hideous thought gripped, the word Salvation hooked my mind. I dissected Sam with a glare. 'You know what we must do, Sam?'

'Report the bastard, soir. Beggin' your pardon.'

'Yes, we must, though not quite yet. Come with me.' I beckoned him and we left by the back entrance.

Through the canopy of trees sunlight anointed Claire's grave; the garden smelled sweet after early morning rain, the summer house's bleached white intense.

Alive with overwhelming elation I spaded out the first clods of earth.

Sam and I worked steadily without a word, certainly not Sam, there only to do my bidding without question. And I repeatedly told myself that one more transfusion might bring her back.

Insane after so many months? Flying in the face of God? I didn't care. Let Him do His worst, for it could never be baser than Schiller's duplicity. And me, wretched soul that I am, wished my daughter back.

Tired and dirty after an hour, Sam and I were able to carry the coffin into the house and rest it on the dining room table. It mattered little that the still damp earth stained the rosewood. Or that the house cried tears of blood over some-thing I dearly longed to convince myself need never have happened?

What darkness raked Schiller's soul? His voice harassed me: 'You gave her your blood. Living blood.'

'Yes, doctor, and you removed it. Why?' An overwhelming urge to strangle him overtook me, a vision of his eyes bulging as he strained for breath.

Eventually I removed the coffin lid expecting to see –

'Sam?' I sought confirmation of what I beheld.

Sam's sharp intake of breath proved I was not hallucinating, that on the satin lining lay Claire's Sunday doll apparently holding hands with the Satur-day doll, smug smiles on their faces. Nothing more.

A sound startled us, something vaguely familiar yet interlaced with a quality unutterably alien. We moved quickly towards the stairs.

Giggles, a name called, so like Eloise shouting: 'Claire.' A laugh so utterly recognisable I wanted to run up those stairs four at a time, reach out, hold her, believe it had all been an offensive joke.

'One for Monday, one for Tuesday –' a voice canted. '...Wednesday... Thursday...'

Sam's steel fingers closed about my upper arm, an unspoken dread making him appear older. I called their names, wondering what Claire would do when she discovered that two of her 'children' were missing.

'Let go, Sam. LET GO!' I shoved him hard against the wall. Ignoring his warnings I called, 'Claire?' before hurrying towards the stairs.

'Thinks I'm not here,' I heard amidst a multitude of whispers, nothing else apparent except for a fleeting glimpse of Claire's favourite scarlet dress, the one she wore to her funeral.

Sam loitered behind me, the sick room smell nauseating. He pointed to letters scrawled in blood on the wall above the chest.

'SCHILLER,' said on a breath as I wondered whose blood it was. My own? Or Claire's?

Sam gestured to the chest. The remaining five dolls had gone.

At my behest, Sam rode like the devil to fetch Schiller on the pretext that I had taken ill. History repeating itself? Not so, because this patient was hardly at death's door.

The doctor and his bag arrived a little after eight. I'd told Sam to direct him to Claire's room where I awaited him, his heavy tread pausing by the chest.

Beyond the window an earlier blue sky resembled the colour of a hearse, the coal dark plumes of cloud horses transmuting into the faces of the dead – my dead. Claire and Eloise.

Bedside manner aside, I witnessed his agitation as he stepped into the room. He glanced at the unmade bed, fully expecting to see me in it.

From the chair, I said without preamble: 'An explanation, Schiller. Enlighten me as to why my daughter is not in her resting place.'

His colour drained: had it not been for the closeness of the dressing table against which he braced himself I think he would have fallen. The bag landed with a slap on the floor.

'I...I...' he stammered.

'Lost for words, Herr Doctor? Eloise and Claire were lost to life.'

He sank onto the stool, head in hands, his answer barely audible, and both shocking, and enlightening. 'I sought only to help you, Leverton, to lessen your grief, to...to hopefully bring her back, to prevent her... *Mein gott*! I failed with your wife, but your daughter... Leverton, I know how you must feel... My transfusion technique – new, vital blood, for diseased blood. By disposing of the diseased blood –'

I threw myself back in the chair. 'You disposed...?' It tumbled to me: Claire's bad blood.

It made sense, my idiot servant witnessing something he had totally misread.

'Leverton,' Schiller said on a sigh, 'it needed a complete transfusion. All I did was to replace some of it with yours hoping it would combat the disease, sadly –'

The truth required no further qualification.

Our eyes met: in his I saw pain. It was the only time I ever trusted Schiller's eyes. And the plausible truth of what he said next.

'I'd hoped to spare you this, but I see now that I must tell you.'

'Tell me what?'

'Leverton, it is your own blood which corrupted both your wife's and your daughter's. I foolishly didn't realise, I overlooked the obvious.'

Intense silence in which words, had there been any, would never have been sufficient to describe, or lend solace to the enormity of guilt.

So, finally it came down to it: Schiller and I, in innocence, are guilty of murder. At least it is how I see it. It will be how Eloise and Claire see it.

The laughter startled Schiller, so high pitched was it, that he whirled to face the door, in all probability recalling his own words.

'Yes, Herr Doctor Schiller,' I said acidly, 'you do remember saying to me, and I quote: "Believe that the dead shall rise, be as one with the living. You gave her your blood. Living blood." Unquote.'

A burning hatred suffused me. I hovered over him, prodded him with my finger. 'Despite my willingness, my need to save Claire you, you Schiller admit negligence. I am a layman when it comes to medicine but you with your Leipzig degree and your charming bedside manner didn't even consider that there may well be a problem. Claire became a guinea pig in order to boost your over-inflated ego. And don't lie, Schiller, you know it's true.'

He said nothing, didn't even take his bag, merely stepped out of the room.

And I hesitated, hearing the sounds on the landing, his screaming, his fists hammering the door, keening cries demanding appeasement...for what? Flying in the face of God?

When I eventually stepped out I stood in blood amidst several scattered dolls whose faces appeared more human. Schiller lay in an awkward heap, his skull and face shattered presumably where he had fallen into the heavy chest.

It is, after all, the most plausible explanation.

To his name inscribed on the wall someone had added:

IN MEMORIAM

I knew where I would find Claire. And Eloise.

Following another visit to the bedroom I hurried outside and made my way to the summerhouse.

They stood hand in hand, Claire in red, Eloise in white. So stark, so utterly beautiful. I whispered their names: they beckoned.

Schiller's large scalpel glinted in my hand, tinged red by the sunset...this time. At least he had unwittingly done me one favour.

It's touch became a caress – of lips belonging to Eloise; the warmth of my daughter's hand as she would stroke my cheek – as I placed it against my throat.

As a family, we should go indoors now, meet the other children: Monday, Tuesday, Wednesday... all the way to Sunday. Thursday and Friday have been damaged beyond repair.

A sacrifice to show us the way? Who knows?

And might it be possible to transfuse a doll with blood? Perhaps Claire will enlighten me one day.

The ground bleeds. The house...bleeds. And will continue to do so, to the depths of love.

In any weather.

Sam will clean up, rid our home of its terrible taint, ensure everything is neat and tidy for our homecoming.

And Schiller? There are two empty graves, but we – Eloise, and I, oh and Samuel – haven't yet made up our minds.

Perhaps we should let the children decide.

REMEMBER ME YESTERDAY

Steve Savile

Death marked the old man; its irresistible charm dancing impatiently behind his wine-dark eyes. He sat at the corner table alone, tearing adverts out of the newspaper laid open before him. A cup of black coffee had gone cold on him while he neatly stacked his scraps of paper.

'I hate all of the commercials,' he grumbled as I slipped into the seat opposite him. 'People who don't know us telling us what we need to make our lives complete. They don't know shit.' An Ebrell watch joined the growing graveyard of commercials set adrift on the tablecloth sea.

Federico had been doing this for as long as I had known him – tearing every advert from every magazine before he deemed them safe for consumption. Not that he ever read them; he simply tore the adverts out and left the naked stories behind. When he was fifteen he had joked that he was a one-man crusade against the evils of *laisse faire*. His wry, slightly self-mocking smile suggested he was well aware how far he had wandered down the Lunatic Road with his obsessions.

He gathered the cuttings up and stuffed them into the pockets of his once designer jacket. The cuffs had frayed, the elbows worn, the patches on the elbows worn. Did he still have boxes of old adverts at home?

'I didn't think you'd come, Caro.' He said it without looking at me.

'Neither did I,' I admitted, and that was the truth. In the eighteen years since I'd last heard Federico's slightly Spanish sounding voice my life had changed. Actually it had become a life; I'd married, divorced and had my son Marcus along the way. But hearing that voice again today when I answered the telephone…Voices carry our secrets. That is what I truly believe: If the eyes are doors into our hearts, where everything we want, crave, desire can be seen in the confusion of colours, the voice is the key to 'us'. A carefully detailed blueprint of the longings, the needs, that are our souls. So much of us, our essence, our history comes wrapped in the sounds our mouths make. But think about it, the voice is something so deliciously ephemeral, changing as it does from morning to night, thickening with emotion, aching with hurt, love, it's all there to hear, our secret selves hidden within the curves and contours of the street map of our souls.

And Federico always had the key to me.

A red-eyed waiter appeared over the shoulder of my window reflection. 'Café latte,' I said to him through the backwards land of the glass. I lit a cigarette and exhaled a beautiful ribbon of blue.

'Have you ever fallen in love, Caroline?' Federico asked when the waiter was gone. Soft jazz whispered around his words. He laid his hands flat on the table, palms up, an old trick. The magician's misdirection showing me there was nothing up his sleeve while the coin was already hidden between his fingers.

'You know I have,' I said softly, looking at the man I used to love, remembering one time, one night, when I finally found the words to say I was all out of love for him. Three a.m., the time when most relationships die in the dark where it's safe because they can't see our eyes. Can't see the truth or the lies. I whispered, 'But I don't love you anymore,' and didn't know if I was talking to him or the memory of him.

'You never did, not enough.'

'Why did you call me, Freddie?' I asked as if I hadn't heard him.

'Because I am dying,' he said simply. 'Because I'm selfish. Because I loved you.'

'So you're putting your house in order?' The words were colder, harsher than I had meant them to be.

'Something like that,' he agreed. I wanted to see him through yesterday's eyes, to see him the way he had been before – before he had taken to wearing this skin that didn't fit. Before the years had carved away his smile, his cheeks, his beautiful mask.

He looked sixty when he wasn't even forty. I looked into his eyes for the accusation, for the blame. And remembered the first time I had seen that wonderful sky. How it had felt that first time, knowing that for just one look that said 'I love you,' I would have been able to fly, fly in those eyes. But, like Icarus, I had flown too close to his sun and melted the wax binding my wings together. With the wax gone the feathers blew away and my flight of teenage love became a free fall into adult loneliness.

His hands twitched on the table. 'I want to ask you something, Caroline. You don't have to say yes, but...' he didn't say any more, didn't have to. His eyes did his talking for him. *If you ever loved me,* they said, *if you ever cared, you won't say no.* 'Take a good look at me, Caro. This is what ol' Papa Death looks like when he comes knocking.' Federico's fingers made the sign of the cross, from forehead to eyes and settling, like a plea for silence, over his lips.

There was a tiredness fogging his eyes now, as if the simple act of talking like this was too much for him.

'Is it cancer?' I asked, putting two and two together and making five. Cancer, the Big C. His post mortem smile seemed to be saying if only life – death – could be that simple. His hands fluttered again, full of nervousness. They cast shadow-wings on the tablecloth. I was struck by the half-formed image of an angel watching over our reunion. Not some all-loving cherub, something more seductive with its sensuous shadow shape, a darker presence blessed with the cold embrace of that endless winter night.

'No,' he said, breaking the angel. He rubbed his eyes. 'No. Listen, Caro. I don't think I have the life left in me to say this more than once. I'm dying but it is not the kind of death I can fight with antibiotics and chemotherapy. I'm dying from here,' Federico touched his temple tenderly, 'to here.' His fingers rested over his heart. 'I'm dying from yesterday all the way into to-day, if that makes any kind of sense.'

'I'm sorry, Freddie,' I said, feeling stupid. 'I haven't got a clue what you are talking about.'

'I'm forgetting myself, my life. You. All the times we spent together, the threads are coming unravelled; it might as well be as if we had never met. As if that time we shared never existed. There are these huge blanks that used to be filled by my life. And with each new memory that slips into the blank spaces, another piece of me dies…'

I tried to put the whole thing into terms I could understand. I'm not a stupid woman but Federico always has had the ability to leave me feeling like an IQ napkin. 'Are you telling me that you've got Alzheimer's?' Jesus, he was less than three months older than I was. The realisation sent cold fingers shivering down the ladder of my spine. 'Is that what's wrong with you?'

'I made a promise to the Thief of Time. I gazed into her eyes and offered everything I had,' he answered cryptically. 'Everything I am, every-thing I was. Now she is collecting her marker.'

'You're talking in riddles, Federico.'

He smiled a sad parody of his old smile. 'The world might love winners, Caro, but she doesn't. Her black smile and her black heart make her a jealous lover. I'm learning how to treat her though. She hates to let the taste of success linger in your mouth. She wants you to know she can always take it all away. I thought I had a chance to win, you know, ever the gambler and now I am dying from yesterday all the days through until today. When the blackness finally catches up, well, then I hope it is painless. A man is the sum of his memories, Caroline. She's taking each and every one from me, one at a time. I'm thirty-eight years old. I've seen a lot of things but I have these holes inside of me that are spreading like cancers, tearing me apart. I can't remember the grin on my own son's face. It's gone. I can't remember what it felt like to dance with his mother in the rain the night he was conceived. I can't remember what she said when we kissed our last goodbye. It's gone… all of it, and I don't mean it is fuzzy, it's gone so thoroughly it might as well never have happened. I need you to help me remember yesterday, Caroline. I want to die knowing who I was.'

He looked at me, the tragedy of his ending life written deep into the sky of his eyes. I so desperately wanted to help him but I didn't have a clue where to start. The Thief of Time? A woman who's dipping into his memories and taking them for her own? It was a Grimm fairy tale. One of Federico's Latin fables. But not Stockholm. Not the Stockholm I had lived in for nearly twenty years. What could I say?

'Have you tried hypnosis?' I said, remembering all of those New Age chat shows littering daytime TV. And then something else occurred to me. 'Maybe you're forgetting for a reason.'

'You just don't listen do you?' Federico said, slamming his hands down on the table suddenly. 'The Thief of Always and Forever is bleeding me dry and you're playing medical join-the-dots.'

'I'm just trying to say that maybe your ghosts won't let you remember, subconscious amnesia. Something like that.'

'I don't have any ghosts,' he said bluntly. 'They've been taken away from me, just like everything else. When I walk through the town, down Vasterlängatan or Sveavagen, I am walking down streets that should be dancing with ghosts of relationships lost, hearts broken, hopes raised, but I'm walking down cold grey stones. The old grey bricks of our school on Vallhal-lavagen, they're dead but I don't see the spirits of us as teenagers haunting the playground. I just don't see it. The bricks and mortar might remain but the memories have gone. It's like being no-one. I could introduce myself to people, "hi, I'm nobody, pleased to meet you."'

'Now you are being ridiculous,' I said, but he wasn't. I tried to put myself in his shoes, project his losses onto my thin shoulders, but it was useless.

'I need you to help me remember,' he said again. I hadn't heard him like this before – this was a whole new Federico. I wasn't sure I liked it.

'But what can I do?'

'Make it come alive for me, the time we spent together. Give me back yesterday.'

I live in a small two-room apartment with a blind cat called Deuteronomy and a view of the big grey mushroom at Stureplan. I love sitting on the cushions in the window, looking out over the city while the light bulbs on the building opposite flash currency rates and stock prices. Sometimes it's raindrops that run down the windowpane, sometimes it's fat white flakes of snow that die on the glass. It's worth the cold and the damp for the summer scents that bring everything to life.

I fell in love with Stockholm the first time I caught the subway. All of these elegant people queuing along the platform's edge, waiting for this rickety old train straight out of the Blitz to come rolling down the tracks. I just stood there on the platform and lost myself in this ocean of colognes. Breathed it in. It was the first time I realised that I was in a foreign city. Everything smelled so rich and wonderful, quite unlike my native New York with its restless heat and its thick blankets of smog and winter snow. It's the kind of thing I take for granted now. One of those simple pleasures.

Raindrops made rivers on the glass while I turned the pages of one of my old photograph albums. I've always been a photo taker. I have a bookcase full of bad photographs of friends, regal snaps of Deuteronomy curled up in the window, tricks of perspective, grey stone streets, snow-laced gargoyles, I even have one that Mikael took of me while we made love. You can't see anything but you can still tell exactly what was happening. Deuteronomy was a ball of contentment listening to the commercials with his usual cattish disinterest. Outside, rainbows were puddling in the gutters, shoppers kicking their feet through the pots of gold at either end. I was thinking about things – people – I hadn't thought about for a long, long time. The sounds from the television changed into a game show: Bingo Lotto. All around the country I imagined people reaching for their purple tickets in the grip of bingo fever. I didn't realise who – or rather, what – I was seeing for a good five minutes.

Veronica Andersson was leaning against the doorway into the building across the street, her beautiful brown eyes looking up at my window. Only it was impossible, it couldn't have been Ronni. The girl looking up at my window was just that, a girl. She couldn't have been a day over fifteen. Veronica was my age; at least she had been the last time I saw her.

Admittedly that was over twenty years ago, but I felt safe in assuming she was still my age. So who? Her daughter? It was possible but what were the odds? Better than my chances of cleaning up on Bingo Lotto, I thought as I raced down the stairs and into the street. Of course, when I hit the pavement Veronica or whoever she was was long gone and I was left looking like a crazy woman chasing ghosts. I had to fight hard to resist the urge to simply grab a passer-by and start babbling about the girl who had been standing in the doorway. Instead, I trudged back up the stairs to my photograph album.

Of course, it occurred to me that she hadn't been there, hadn't been looking up at my window. That made the most sense, and it didn't mean I was going crazy either, just that I had been so busy thinking about being back at school with Federico and the others I simply saw a resemblance on some stranger's face and blew it up to the size of an honest to God Peter Pan clone peeking through my window.

But something Federico had said came back to me: 'I made a promise,' that's what he said. 'I made a promise to the Thief of Time. I gazed into her eyes and offered everything I had. Everything I am, everything I was. Now she is collecting her marker.'

I looked down at the photograph of Veronica I had in my lap, at her eyes and found myself sinking into a dream I wasn't ready for.

I sat at the same table in Café Muren with three packets of photographs neatly stacked beside the ashtray. I'd actually given up smoking two years before, but I needed something to do with my hands and holding a thin coffin nail seemed as good as anything. I wasn't really sure what I was going to do, sure I had a few ideas about flashback therapy, offering Federico a picture of the old school, of my old coffee cup with the 70s psychedelic swirls, the one he broke trying to juggle it along with two oranges; he had been trying to impress Louise and Karin. I smiled at the memory but then a strange feeling of selfishness settled over me; how easily I could recall all of this mundane childhood stuff and there was Federico who couldn't very well remember what day it was. I stopped smiling.

When he came in through the door he looked more than a day sicker. He had a bundle of magazines under his arm, glossies with those tear off perfume samples and bulimic models. He sank into the seat opposite me. The nuts and bolts holding his face in place had loosened another notch and folds of loose skin were wrinkling up like the chins of a Pekinese pooch.

'I thought I saw Veronica last night,' I said, offering it like bait.

'Veronica?' was all he said, but it was enough for me to know that whatever memories had anchored Veronica to Federico were gone. It gave me somewhere to start. I picked up the first packet of photographs and thumbed through them until I saw a candid snap of Veronica and Nic K. slow dancing in the dining hall. I teased it out and lay it on the table between us. Federico studied both of the faces in the photograph without the tiniest flicker of recognition in his eyes.

'That's Veronica,' I said. 'Don't you recognise her?'

He shook his head. 'Pretty little thing,' I thought I saw a hint of a smile when he said that.

'We were all in school together,' I said softly and began to go through the photographs one at a time, feeding him with memories that should have been his own. The first one was of me on stage at the graduation ceremony. There was no real order to the pictures, I was working on a kind of hit and hope philosophy, throwing out event after event purely on the basis that the BIG things would break away bigger chunks of the amnesia or whatever it was and give Federico back bigger segments of his past. So after the graduation it was a picture of him leaning against the door of a blue two door '57 Volvo Coupe with a spectacular view of Stockholm filling the background. There was more to the picture than what was shown.

It had been a Friday night filled with mosquitoes and saxophones. We'd driven up to Vanity Hill with the top down, parked on the side of the road and laid our blanket out. He'd tried to teach me the names of some of the major constellations but I kept joking about seeing my uncle's face in the clouds and that my dad had sent him to spy on us. It was difficult to get a fix on my Ursa Minor's and Major's with a rather cumulous member of the family breathing down my neck. I wasn't used to drinking back then and the Chablis had gone straight to my head. I wasn't drunk, but I was on the way and when we started to kiss things just started to happen and instead of slowing them down, stopping them, I started chasing them. It was a natural progression; soon we were exploring each other for the first time. It was the night we both lost our virginity and I could tell all that from a stupid photo of a beat-up Volvo and Federico's shit eating grin.

The next photograph was of this huge Cat In The Hat character called Simon, whose fingers were decked out in gold and diamante. Next to his smile and his pearly white teeth all that gold was as dull as daytime t.v.

We went through five years that morning, with the waiter topping up our coffee cups frequently. Talked about things that I remembered and he didn't. Had a quiz after two years, the highs and lows of a teenage life laid bare. Twenty questions. No points for wrong answers. No questions repeated. If you don't know the answer go on to the next question. The usual quiz show stuff. Federico scored three points. It was a start.

Deuteronomy woke me by sitting on the left side of my face. The night was shadow boxing on the bedroom wall. Everything had the cold Stockholm touch to it, the oak floor kissed like a razor as I walked across it, drawn to the window.

I'd known she would be there, looking up at my window. There was something horribly inevitable about seeing her fifteen-year-old face tilted up to look at me. I rested my hands on the window-ledge, my weight on my hands. The photograph album was still open on the side, a shot of Veronica in her pale floral dress caught in the sun. I looked at the girl in the street, back at the girl in the photo album. A shiver danced rung by rung down the ladder of my spine. It was her. The girl in the street was Veronica, the Veronica of twenty years ago, the Veronica I'd grown up with who had somehow stopped growing old, just like Peter Pan, and now here she was, on my doorstep the exact same week that Federico walked back into my life. Coincidence?

I read somewhere that there was no such thing as coincidence, fate, kismet, whatever you want to call it. But did that discount *meaningful* coincidence? A lover unheard from for twenty years and the sudden sighting of an ex-best friend from high school in the same week? Well, no. But... An ex-best that has somehow arrested the ageing process? Trapped herself in a bubble of 1979?

The rain didn't seem to be touching her. It had to be a trick of perspective and bad light, but it had the cold hand of fear clutching at my stomach just the same. There she was, standing in the rain, bone dry.

Deuteronomy rubbed himself up against my leg, purring deep in his throat.

I dressed slowly, warmly, in jeans and a baggy blue sweatshirt. Then I took my time lacing my sneakers. I didn't hurry because I knew she'd still be standing there not getting wet in the rain when I walked out of the door.

I took one last glance at the photographs; saw the photograph of Federico leaning against his blue Volvo that I had put back into the album a few hours before, and walked down the stairs and into the street, trying for the life of me to remember the name of the hill where we had made love that first time.

I ran out into the middle of the road like a mad woman. Three a.m., Stockholm, an in-between time, where the nightlife is giving way to the newspaper deliverers and the early morning smells of cinnamon hanging warmly in the air. The lights of the all night sandwich bar on the corner were on, a couple of star-crossed lovers eating pastrami on rye and supping cola, prolonging the night and angling towards a bed somewhere in the city, either together or alone.

I stopped walking two feet shy of the curb, close enough to see the lack of lines on Veronica's sad face. She seemed to be staring right through me as if it was me that was the ghost, not her.

'Ronni?' I whispered, barely above a breath. 'Is that you?'

Her eyes came down from looking at the angels and saw me for the first time in twenty years. It *was* her. I don't know what I expected, that she would open her mouth to talk and there would be *nothing*, no words, nothing. That she would suddenly spill the secrets of immortality and young looking skin.

That she would turn out to be someone else and this was all some huge paranoid joke I was playing out at my own expense.

'Caroline,' she said, dubiously, almost as if she didn't recognise me. 'You're all grown up.'

I nearly laughed. It was such an innocuous thing to say, yet it summed everything up neatly. I was all grown up and somehow she was still fifteen and locked in eternal puberty.

It was the strangest sensation, being face to face with my own apparition, my own Ghost of Christmas past come to take me around the city by night. I don't remember Scrooge being soaked to the skin in his story though. Maybe Dickens was a kinder God than mine, or maybe I was less of a character than old Ebanezer; less rounded, less unique, less worthy of creature comforts. So I cried tears of rain. I had no answer to Veronica's almost accusation. It was a very simple truth; I was all grown up. That's what twenty years do to a girl. They wrap her up in a silk cocoon like an ugly caterpillar and give birth to a woman, sometimes beautiful, sometimes plain. The trick is forgetting that first skin that was childhood and all of its growing pains and embracing the wings we need to fly through the rest of our lives.

Oh Jesus, I'm starting to sound like one of those damned self-help novels they sell in airports. You have to fall in love with yourself before you can fall in love with anyone else. Yeah, right. My mother hated every second of every day she spent with the abusive son of a bitch that helped hatch me, hated his kisses as much as she hated his kicks, yet I was surrounded by love while I grew up. How? Simple, there was no trick. All of the hatred he directed at her, she absorbed, amplified, and gave back to me as love. Overcompensated for the bastard who just happened, by biological defect, to be my daddy. But she believed everything he said about her; I could see it in her eyes. The haunted look of a woman who believes she is worthless. Even when she was dying all she could do was apologise.

'But she loved you,' Ronni said, as if she had found a way inside my head.

'What?'

'Your mother, she loved you. You must know that. Every time he hit her, it was thinking about you that gave her the strength to get back up again... without you she would have given up a long time before, just laid down and died.'

So, I made it worse? I wanted to say it, but she reached out, placing her thumbs over both of my eyes like some faith healer trying to make me see again. 'It is the same with Federico,' she whispered. 'Your simply being there gives him the strength to go on.'

I tried to take some kind of comfort from what she said, but I couldn't because if my simply being there had caused my mother so much more pain what was I doing to Federico?

'I was forty once, like you are now,' she said, suddenly. 'And then he came back into my life. Said he'd forgotten nearly everything except me. Said some thief had stolen his past but it was a lie, he is the only thief, feeding himself off everything he never had the guts to experience. Now he is feeding off you... What have you given him? Tell me.' Ronni's thumbs pressed into my eyes, hard enough to hurt.

I jerked away, trying to break her hold on me but her thumbs kept pressing as if they were trying to squeeze the truth out of me. 'Please, you're hurting me,' I said, holding her wrists and trying to pull my head back. 'I haven't given him anything. We've just talked a few times. He hasn't asked me for anything.' It was a lie, and I knew it as soon as it came off my tongue. A big fat lie that had come to life all by itself. Of course he had asked me for something, he'd asked me to give him his past back, his memories. What had I given him? Nothing really. A few images. The photograph of the blue two door Volvo '57 Coupe taken on... on... I couldn't remember the name of the hill, the place where we had made love for the first time, where I had lost my virginity to Freddie... 'Oh, Sweet God in heaven,' I whispered, realising it was gone. That there was a little black spot where it had been.

'What have you given him?' Ronni hissed again. 'Tell me.'

'I told him how we made love the first time... and now... I can't remember... it's gone... like it never happened. I can see the car, it was a blue car...with red leather seats... but I can't remember the place... I can't remember where he laid me down... oh God, oh God, help me... help me...'

'Take your time, think about it, try to build the picture... try to remember. Panic is the enemy. Fear will steal more of yourself than you've already lost. Just try to relax, let the memories wash over you like water.'

I swallowed a breath, tried to imagine I was a pebble in the river of my dreams, tried to picture memories like swift flowing water, to let them wash over me, roll over me, sweep me away, and they did for a while, from childhood days into school days, faces, people, places, memories, all of them like icy water running through my veins, until the torrent formed a whirlpool around one face, Federico's face. It was like a dam, the thoughts stopped flowing and instead began to churn and fold in on themselves, frothing up white water and black spots. Things I should have known, had known... had told Freddie over the table in Café Muren but couldn't remember now.

'It's gone,' I said softly, giving in.

'Try,' she hissed. 'Try.'

'It's no good,' I said pathetically. 'It's gone.'

'Then I pity you,' Veronica Andersson whispered, her eyes full of the

28

sadness of knowing, understanding. 'Because you'll never get it back, and now he has his hooks in you, you're just going to lose more and more of yourself, until you're a child like me, reduced to haunting doorways at night for fear someone from your past might recognise you and soon enough you'll find yourself wishing for Childhood's End, not that it can ever come. You're Peter Pan's plaything now...'

The perfect sky was torn by a fork of dry lightning.

I looked at the woman reflected in the window of Café Muren. I wasn't sure if I was trying to convince myself that there were any visible changes in the face that looked back or not. Not that the glass offered any details, no wrinkles or laughter lines just the wide sweep of features that made up my face. And it was my face, the one I had grown up with, the one I had been wearing a few days before when I'd met Federico tearing out his collection of advertisements and stacking them neatly – or near as damn it the same, a little voice niggled. I had stopped paying attention to the details a long time ago so I couldn't swear that everything was exactly the same as it had always been. It looked the same to me, maybe a little more haunted around the eyes.

Every journey begins with a single step, right? It doesn't matter how far you are going, there is always one step at the beginning that sets the whole thing off. I pushed open the Café door and took that long step over the threshold into Federico's world.

He was sitting at what I was already beginning to think of as his table, thumbing through a copy of yesterdays' *Dagens Nyheter*, his fingers black with newsprint. An oversized cup of black iced coffee and a wedge of Alabama fudge were off to the side, both untouched. He was waiting for me yet he didn't look up as I eased myself into the seat opposite his.

'I saw Ronni last night,' I said when he didn't look up. I wanted to shock him into some kind of reaction. He looked up slowly to the sound of tearing paper, his sky blue eyes overcast, filled with rain.

'No you didn't,' he said simply. 'You saw what *she* wanted you to see but you didn't see Veronica.'

'How do you know I didn't see her?' I asked, trying unsuccessfully to keep the edge out of my voice. 'Were you there?' When he didn't answer I nodded to myself, satisfied. 'No, you weren't were you.'

'I didn't need to be there this time. I was with her when she died. I held her hand in a cold hospital ward while her husband was off somewhere feeling sorry for himself. Her hand was in mine when the life finally left her eyes. Do you understand now? You couldn't have seen her because she died five years ago. You saw something, I don't doubt that, but it wasn't

Veronica.'

That stopped me. 'No,' I said, clinging to the image of the young girl standing in the rainy night. 'No,' I repeated. 'She isn't dead... I saw her last night... she was... younger...'

In a few days the world had stopped making sense.

'She's dead, Caro.'

I desperately wanted to believe him, needed to believe that he wasn't some kind of memory stealing vampire, that he was the same old Freddie he'd always been, but I didn't know who I could believe anymore. Last night everything Ronni had said had seemed so *believable* and now, looking at the pain in Federico's eyes, I couldn't see how he could be lying. 'So *who* did I see last night? Tell me that much, please Freddie. I *want* to believe you. I really do.'

He closed his eyes, looking for the strength somewhere inside him to say the words I wanted to hear. When he opened them again the clouds had gone. There was nothing but endless cobalt blue sky. 'You met her, the Thief of Time. You met the demon that is killing me and you fell for her lies, didn't you?'

'No, I – '

'Please don't lie to me, Caro. She's persuasive. Believable. She has a way of getting what she wants. I won't hold it against you.'

'Yes, then... but only because I don't understand.' I said weakly. It was more the truth than he could know. 'Tell me so I can.'

'Her name is Corimera. No, that's not true, that's what she told me to call her. Her name is something else. She knew I understood the rules, that names hold power, true names, so she gave me a lie because she knew I wanted to believe her. You see, I loved her. But she doesn't care about that, about love. She only wants what she can take, not what can be given freely. There is no power in receiving, only in taking. The more she takes from me, the more of my spirit she absorbs, the more about her I understand. It's like a two-way mirror, I don't see everything and nothing is very clear, but I do see outlines, ghosts. I'm not the only one she has done this to, I know that now. To one lover she is Hera, to another Helene, Sarah, she is whoever they need her to be, but her real name, her given name, is Death. She touches all of our lives, draws them to a close like one of the Fates cutting the thread of life. She found me in the street and made me love her because I had nothing else in my life left that was worth loving.'

I took his hand in mine, turned it palm up. Both his lifeline and his loveline were broken by an intricate motorway of cracks that had been bled over by newsprint. 'Go on,' I coaxed gently.

'It was after my military service, I was working as a cameraman for

SVT 1. It was nothing glamorous, mostly news coverage. A fire at a youth club in Göteborg. A prison breakout. Skinheads causing trouble. Bus strikes in Stockholm and a train crash. Point the camera and let the loss of life do the talking. An idiot could have done it but the thing was, it was me doing it. It was me pointing the camera and it began to affect me. If you stare long enough into the abyss, right? After the fire, having to film the faces of dead kids being carried out of the gutted building, I wanted to be as far away from the camera lens as possible... as far away from real life as I could manage... I wrote poetry for a while, and hung around coffee shops pretending I was *tres chic*, but it was either drivel or haunted by the faces of burn victims.' He looked at me then, and I could feel every ounce of his pain. I'd seen the television coverage of the fire; who hadn't. Sixty-six kids dead at a Christmas party because of a faulty fire alarm. 'So I just dropped out. I started drinking. A lot. Too much too ever have been healthy. I wasn't looking for answers, I was on a quest for oblivion, and that was harder to find than any answer I might have gone looking for.'

'It wasn't your fault,' I said for want of something to say, some comfort to offer. He didn't seem to hear me.

'Because they were always there, even when I was drunk. Their faces, those dead kids staring up at me. And when I was drunk it was worse because they started talking to me. I just couldn't cope. I wasn't strong enough to kill myself. I think I thought that would only bring them closer, a mixed up kind of resurrection, not them brought back from the dead but me brought back to them... so I just drunk myself into a perpetual stupor while my life crashed and burned.'

The red-eyed waiter brought me an unasked for café latte and left us alone again.

'That was where she found me, in the gutter. I was living out of bins, sleeping nights beneath the railway arches of the Central Station or in the amusement rides in Gröna Lund. It was off-season so no one was around to chase me off. It was raining. I remember that. She likes the rain... I'd passed out beneath the canopy of the carousel with my arm wrapped around a unicorn's ankles... She was beautiful, her black hair hanging in wet ringlets down her forehead, her skin like alabaster...' He drifted in his telling of the story, caught up in the memory of meeting the woman he called Death. 'I thought my heart was going to burst in my chest just from looking at her. It was like I was looking at a part of myself that had always been missing... I don't know how else to explain it. With her to fill my eyes there wasn't enough room for dead kids... Without a word she held her hand out to me and I took it. No thunderbolts. No lightning. We walked beneath the Ferris Wheel and between the Ghost Train and the Tunnel of Love. I didn't care where she was taking me. I didn't want to know. I just wanted to be with her.'

'So why do you call her the Thief of Time?' I asked then, sure that there was a rational, reasonable explanation for Veronica still being fifteen and Federico being closer to sixty. He looked at me as if to say: *are you stupid?*

'Look at me, Caro. What do you see?'

'I see you,' I answered obtusely, I knew what he was getting at but I wasn't about to give it to him, I wanted to hear him say it. No easy get outs, no helpful misunderstandings. His words; his truth; his lies.

'No you don't,' he said, his lip curling. 'You see an old man. That's why I call her the Thief of Time, because that is what she does. She steals every day, every memory, and leaves behind the husk, all withered and shrivelled like a piece of old fruit. That's why. Just look at me. Look at me, look me in the eye and tell me I am *not* wasting away. Not ageing faster than that tangerine in your fruit bowl.'

I met his gaze, then broke the contact.

'Can't do it, can you?' he mocked.

'You're sick, Freddie. I don't know what is doing it to you, but I find it hard to believe some supernatural entity is bleeding the years out of you...'

His fingers drummed on the tablecloth. He didn't seem aware of what they were doing, how loud they had become. 'I never said she was anything more than a woman, Caro. You said that. I said she was the Thief of Time, Death herself, you said supernatural. You said impossible.' He started coughing; a shallow cough that couldn't seem to dislodge whatever it was that was filling his throat.

'Freddie? Are you okay?' I asked anxiously. The coughing fit didn't want to stop. After half a minute, more, he brought up blood. Flecks of the stuff sprayed from his lips to speckle the palms of his hands. 'Jesus, Freddie, what's happening?' I was up and around the table but there was nothing I could do except wait it out. I rubbed and patted stupidly on his back. People were beginning to look. Someone shouted: 'He's choking!' but he wasn't. He hadn't eaten anything. Then it struck me; I hadn't seen Federico eat a thing in all of the time we'd spent together since our reunion. He always ordered food and ended up leaving it untouched.

The red-eyed waiter pushed passed me, wrapped his arms around Federico's wasit and started heaving against his stomach, trying to force whatever it was that was choking him out. One, two, three. Quick jerks. Something red, glossed over with blood, spat out of his lips and skittered across the floor and he was left gasping for breath in the waiter's arms. Everyone was looking at Freddie. Not me. I was looking at the red thing that had come out of his mouth. It was blood definitely, and some kind of film, almost like an egg without the shell, the film meshed with white lines. While I stared at it, the white lines became thin spidery legs that twitched, stretching the mucus-covering that had eased the passage of whatever it was into this world. I tried to tell myself it was raw tissue from Freddie's throat and stomach lining but it wasn't. The legs finally tore the membranous sack and clenched the air, finding the strength they needed to support the things' golf ball sized body, and then it was skittering away into the darkness beneath another diner's table. I wanted to scream so badly there was no way not to. I reached out for the table. Needed it to keep me from falling. I couldn't have seen what I had just seen.

I couldn't have seen Ania Chaborik's face on that... that... thing.

I couldn't have...

'Caro? Caro?' It was Federico, wiping the blood from his lips as he reached out to steady me. I shook his hand off, backed away, turned and ran out of the cafe and into the rain.

'What the hell was that... that... thing?' I said bluntly. There were two ways of looking at it, and over the last three days I'd stared at both pretty hard. The first was that none of it had happened, no phonecall, no Federico, no Veronica, no blood-spider, that I was the victim of one ugly hallucination but I knew that wasn't true. So the other angle was that *all* of it was real. That was so much worse than merely seeing things.

He'd come looking for me after I left my machine to pick up all his calls. In each message he sounded progressively more desperate. I don't know why, but I liked that. The clock on the wall had stuck at three. It had been like that for days but I didn't have a spare battery to get it going again. Every time the phone rang Deuteronomy would start brushing up against it, trying to dislodge the handset from its cradle with his paw. Dumb cat didn't realise the kind of trouble that was waiting on the other end of the line. After three days the calls finally stopped. I thought he'd given up. I was wrong. An hour later Federico was pounding on my door. Hard. Demanding that I answer. Finally, I gave in. I opened the door for him.

Now he was pacing the hardwood floor of my lounge, making cats cradles with his fingers. He looked like Hell... No that wasn't true. He looked a little better than Hell. He'd looked like Hell when I ran out on him, now, if anything, he looked slightly worse.

He didn't offer me a smooth lie; it was too late for that. He looked at me with eyes that were as dark and broody as a thunder-sky. 'You know what it was,' he said, rubbing at his chin. 'It was someone... a friend... I can't remember who... it was my memories of them. Gone.' He threw his hands up helplessly.

I got up from my seat and went over to the window to stare out into the street. I half expected Veronica to be sheltered in the doorway opposite but, as Federico had pointed out when he finally calmed down enough to talk, it wasn't raining. A steady stream of cars, Volvos and Nissans of each and every colour and hue, moved in a metal snake down the road, a red city bus making the rattle at the tail.

'You don't seriously expect me to buy into that, do you?' I said, doing my best Gillian Anderson impression. I didn't turn around to look at him. I didn't need to, thanks to the light he was reflected in the glass like a spectre overlapping the street below.

'That's how it happens,' he muttered, still pacing. 'I have no control over it you know... she chokes it out of me... I can tell its going to happen a while before it does. I find myself thinking about someone a lot. Not just how they look, things they say, everything. It's as if she is leafing through the memories one by one, weeding the person out of my mind, then when she's done, everything is out, it's as if they become a hairball or something... you know, they just have to get out and I start choking...until I cough them out... That, back there in the café, that was nothing... I thought I was going to die the first time she stole someone from me.'

He was telling me the truth, or at least he thought he was, that much was painfully obvious.

'You've got to help me, Caroline. I can't take much more of this.'

That much was also obvious, just from looking at him. His eyes seemed to be falling into his skull, the cavities around them were so pronounced. Actually, it was as if he'd taken to wearing blue mascara on the skin beneath his eyes, or someone had punched him hard enough to bruise the entire eye socket of both eyes. And his hands... the folds of skin hung from his fingers like gloves that were far too big for his birdlike hands.

Prognosis terminal, Mr. Chuavas. Two, three days at most, I'd say, if you asked me, I thought darkly. Two or three days.

'How?' I asked. 'How can I help you? What can I do?'

'Tell me stories, tell them fast. I need to know my life. I need to share your memories, pretend they are my own. I'm running out of things for her to take, Caro. There isn't much of me left...' *Two or three days,* I said to myself. 'I need some fake plastic memories to buy me time... I don't know what else to do, how else to fight her...'

'Jesus... I need a drink,' I said then, going through to the kitchen to brew a jug of strong black coffee, Swedish style. Thick enough to stand a spoon in. Freddie stayed in the lounge. 'Put some music on,' I called through. 'This is going to be a long night.' He grunted something and after a minute

REMEMBER ME YESTERDAY

Ani Difranco was telling us all about her Little Plastic Castle. I got the joke after a minute. *Goldfish have no memory and the little plastic castle is a surprise every time...* 'Funny, Freddie,' I said, pouring out my first cup of the night ahead. Corkscrews of steam curled up under my nose as I carried the two cups through. 'So you haven't lost your sense of humour, huh?'

He managed a smile. 'I just remember you loving that damned song... Used to hum it everywhere you went.'

We sat down facing each other, no putting it off anymore. I reached over to the bookcase for one of my many photograph albums and flipped it open on Marcus's baby face. I turned the page quickly. I didn't want my son getting mixed up in this. Besides, Marcus was no business of Federico's. None. Five years back in five pages and there was Freddie leaning against his car on that hill... I stared at the picture trying for the life of me to remember what was special about it. Nothing. It was gone.

I looked for a different photograph, one I knew something about. It was of me and Louise Langeby smiling over the top of huge ice cream sundaes dripping with cola sauce and mint green liqueur. I smiled slightly, remembering just how incredibly competitive Louise had been about everything. In the photograph her hair was pulled up in its usual businesslike ponytail, her face *sans* makeup, pretty but nothing special. I smiled inwardly, wondering what Louise would think of me; people in glass houses shouldn't throw stones, right? I rested my fingertip on the photograph and began my long night as Scheherazade, telling stories to save a life.

'This was taken a year after we graduated high school, in an ice cream parlour in Gamla Stan. Wonderful ice cream. We were celebrating because Louise had just landed herself a job as a copy editor with Bonniers.' I stopped thinking about the words I was saying, found myself visualising them instead, reliving the memories...

The inside of the ice cream parlour was cold even though the paraffin heater was pumping out warmth. It had been a stupid idea coming for ice cream in January. Snow lined the street and banked up against the window like a scene from a Christmas card. Louise was really getting on my nerves, all of her talk about Bonniers this and Bonniers that, and the way she curled her lip up whenever she deigned to think about my own fledgling career as a makeup artist at Face. Still, the ice cream *was* good.

'Tell me about our break-up,' Federico interrupted, breaking the illusion. I looked at the clock, trying to get some sense of how long I had been under, but it was still stuck at three. The neons out in the street prevented the moon from giving any hints.

But it wasn't the moon I was looking at.

It was Federico.

F20

36

Only Federico.

Always Federico.

A thin dribble of blood was running from the corner of his mouth, losing itself in the cracks of his chin. He didn't seem to be aware of it so I reached out to wipe it away but his hand snaked out and grabbed mine, his grip surprisingly strong, hurt. 'Don't,' he hissed, refusing to let go of my hand even when he felt the urge to move fade from my muscles.

I didn't know what to say. I looked up from the ribbon of blood into his dead eyes. I was wrong, the sky had never lived in them. A flat rolling emptiness of oblivion consumed them. That was all there was to him. Emptiness. Oblivion.

'Tell me about our break-up,' he repeated harshly.

I shook my head, no. His fingers dug into my wrists. Twisting. 'Tell me, Caro. You know you will so don't make me hurt you.' I couldn't break his hold, no matter how much I wanted to. 'Needless pain is such a waste of good suffering.' The more pressure he put on my wrists the more vehemently I shook my head. But I couldn't help myself, I started *thinking* about it…

The room was dark, for once not bathed in moonlight. Shadows cast by the limbs of the old tree in my parents' garden danced on the white wall. I watched them trying to put some sort of message into their movement; a subtext about the decline of civilisation and the end of Empire, or something equally bogus. Free spirits that they were, the trees were having nothing to do with it. 'I don't love you anymore,' I said at last, knowing he couldn't see my eyes. We'd made love less than an hour before. I felt cheap. Dirty. Used. I could never have said the words if he had been looking at me. The darkness gave me the strength to say what we both knew: It was over.

'You were it, Caro.' Federico's voice was consumed by sadness. Blood was running from both nostrils now. No longer a thin trickle, it was bleeding into the collar of his shirt. He looked as if he had been shot in the neck. 'You were *the* one. My North, my South, my East and my West… and you *left* me…'

It really was like an ugly hallucination, the way the past kept overlaying the present with its painful memories.

Something was beginning to happen inside me; I could feel it. Not like Freddie had explained it, not some kind of hairball at the back of my throat. It was in my stomach, a severe cramp, like a period pain but so much more *intense*. It felt like my womb was on fire and my ovaries were about to burst. *And spill bloody red spiders onto the floor,* that damned voice goaded.

'You left me,' he repeated softly.

I had started crying; I don't remember when. I *hurt* so much. Inside and out. 'I'm sorry,' I managed, trying to curl up into a foetal ball even though he still had my hands. 'I'm sorry.'

'Sweet Caroline,' he soothed, lowering me to the floor. One moments softness exchanged for a brutal kick to my belly. A second kick, crunching into my breastbone. 'You were always the one... It had to be you... I'm sorry, Caro. If... If I hadn't loved you, it wouldn't hurt so much...'

I sobbed, breaking.

I thought I was going to throw up; felt something soft brushing up against me. Deuteronomy. I tried to push him away but my body wouldn't answer my mind.

Something sounded, a banging, a knock at the door: 'Don't go away now,' Federico whispered, brushing back my hair tenderly before he went to answer the knocking. I tried to move but it was impossible. So I just lay there in a ball, wishing I were dead while the spider of reality crawled inside my ear and whispered: 'Whyyyyy don't youuuu kill him?'

It was laughable; I couldn't even move and despite his outward frailty there was steel moving that loose flesh of Federico's. I didn't have a hope in Hell.

There were voices but I couldn't hear what they were saying, not at first. I could just make out Federico's but the others... some female, I guessed before I finally blacked out.

A ring of faces surrounded me when I came too. Federico's dead eyes looking down paternally, Veronica's still clouded with fairy dust and angels. But there were others. Faces I hadn't seen since high school. Ania, Louise, Neha, Mary and Elisa, each looking at me as if I had somehow betrayed them. Each face impossibly young, every eye haunted by the kind of emptiness only death can bring. They crowded around me like so many spiders chittering over their prey.

Come to feast.

That was when I felt it; the first dribbles of blood trailing down the inside of my thigh. The pain in my womb, already unbearable, doubled, trebled. I could feel, *literally* feel, something crawling down through the lips of my vagina, hungry to be out in the world. I was screaming and they were all leaning over me and cooing, urging me to give birth.

I was wrong.

There was a lot of blood.

I felt Federico's fingers on my temples, soothing, gentling. And I felt Federico's fingers inside my head, picking through my memories, weeding them out, plucking out what he wanted, what he needed.

When it came, the memory was born in the same kind of mucus-covered spider that Freddie had coughed up. This one wore a man's face, older, it had meant something to me once but now there was nothing, a blank space where this man had been in my life.

Deuteronomy watched the blood-slicked spider as it crawled down my leg, his eyes feral, bright. Instinct took over. The cat lunged, no time for playing with his food. One clawed paw snagged the spider and his open mouth came down instinctively to eat.

Federico was screaming but he couldn't move with anything approaching the speed or agility of the cat. Deuteronomy finished eating the small spider and turned to consider the old man screeching at him with disinterested eyes.

Good boy, I urged, biting back on the pain as a second memory began its journey down the birth canal. *Now do it again...* Anything was better than this monster I used to call a friend swallowing my life, my memories, whole... But Deuteronomy wasn't going to be doing it again. The thing that was Federico saw to that. He took my cat in his hands and began to pull, cracking his ribcage then splitting it open with burrowing fingers, fishing the memory out before it had had a chance to dissolve in Deuteronomy's stomach acids. Dropping the cat he stuffed the bloody spider into his mouth and swallowed it whole, licking his fingers as if to savour a particularly rare delicacy.

I didn't have the strength to cry any more than I was already crying. Black holes were opening up inside my skull. Holes where people had lived once upon a time. One by one the Real Thief of Time delivered my memories into the world, memories of Ania and Elisa, Louise, Mary and Neha, the mucus-covered spiders into each of their mouths, bringing back a part of themselves that the Thief had already stolen. They were feeding themselves off me. A swarm of those blood-slicked spiders skittered all over the floor. They just kept pouring out of me, a lifetime of memories. It didn't matter that I didn't know who they were anymore, I knew they were feeding off me like vampires, claiming back a month or a year of their stolen age with each swallow.

What they didn't take Federico devoured, swallowing the chitinous memories down like a glutton, licking his fingers after each mouthful – not to enjoy, I realised distantly, but to drain, to make sure he got each and every last drop of memory soaked blood from them.

And with each one another line was erased from his face, another tendon firmed beneath the slowly tightening skin.

He drank from me until I was empty.

I lay there on the floor, waiting to die.

But it wasn't going to be that easy.

They were gone, whoever they were, like ghosts, phantoms, things that never were, never would be.

I was alone with the emptiness inside my head. The blackness that used to house laughter and friendship, lovers and sadness. Everything around me was strange. The floor on which I bled, I'd never seen it before. The music still playing on the stereo, likewise, sounds I had never heard before.

I crawled onto my knees, ignoring the bloody mess of a cat someone had slaughtered. I didn't recognise the face I saw reflected in the window. A young girl of fourteen or fifteen surrounded by a halo of dawn's early light. It had to be me but I could have been looking at anyone. Looking at myself I felt the first cramps of period pain coming on. Everything felt stiff. Sore.

Had I been raped? The thought sent a chill shivering down the length of my spine. There was enough blood. And it hurt enough... Oh Jesus... Is that what had happened?

I touched myself tentatively, but it was impossible to tell. Everything felt raw.

I closed my eyes, searching for something inside; some memory that would help make sense of things. Nothingness stretched back for years and years where memories had been, back until it faltered at the foot of a flickering flame... A face... A young boy...

Marcus...

That was his name...

Marcus.

My son.

I looked at myself in the window again. The girl I saw looking back was too young to have a son yet the memory remained, stronger than anything else. More real. Marcus, my son. The one soul I had truly loved in this life of mine. My one. My North, my South, my East and my West.

Somehow, I understood, without knowing how I did, he had the key to me.

Whoever they were, they'd left me one thing, one guiding light, for a reason. Only it wasn't a light, in the same way that cancer isn't a light, or AIDS, or cot death. They are ways out, but they aren't the light at the tunnels' mouth. His face in my memory was more like the darkest spot in the heart of a black hole, sucking up light and sound and everything else greedily. He was everything to me.

I staggered out into the early morning rain, not knowing where I was going, only that I had to find him, find my son and beg him to be my Scheherazade, to tell me my life over a thousand and one nights, to tell me everything: who I am, who I was, who I will be.

The cold hit me, the bone deep chill.

It didn't matter. I was going to find him and he was going to give me the truth no matter what the cost.

Lovers were huddled in the doorway across the street from the apartment, one impossibly handsome Latino with the whole sky reflected in his eyes, the other an elegant mistress with raven black hair and deepset haunting eyes. Their fingers intertwined as they watched me pass, a lost soul in a big city of equally lost souls. They smiled gently, like mother and father watching their baby take her first steps, nodding encouragingly as I looked up and down the street, trying to taste my son on the wind.

Like they say, every journey begins with a single step. Putting one foot in front of the other I began walking.

THE DESTROYERS

Paul Finch

As the end of our time neared, it was written unto many stones, most readily in that ancient land of apostate kings, the Distant East, that Man would spill a tide of blood unlike any known since that scourge of tribes, Attila. Eager to partake of this feast, the godless things that swim in dark and unseen places …
Childeric
Anno Domini 1099

Jerusalem – the navel of the world, the sacred city of Christians, Jews and Moslems alike – might have been worth the wearying journey to reach it, had its alleys not swarmed with flies, its squares and courts not lain under a vast litter of the hacked and the mutilated and the dead.

In any normal time, the sight of the sun – a ball of orange flame high on the rugged flanks of Mount Zion, or shimmering through the green canopies of lemon and fig trees in the lush gardens of Gethsemane – might stop the surliest man in his tracks and make him draw breath, but now that sun was lost in a haze of acrid smoke, and the sky, the little of it visible, fluttering with ravens.

'They said the Church of the Sepulchre was once destroyed,' the boy muttered, 'by the mad Caliph Al-Hakim. But that it was raised to glory again, by a Viking … Harald Hardraada, in the pay of Byzantium. I thought it would be an astounding place to visit.'

'It was, Wulfric,' said the man after a moment. 'Didn't you feel that?'

And to some extent that was true. They'd both of them been inside that great and holy place, been witness in person to its many coloured marbles and rich murals. The boy had been shocked, though, that even there the people of the city had failed to find sanctuary from the crusader army, and almost as one, had fallen beneath a flailing storm of blades and mattocks.

Even there, on that very site where Jesus himself had lain entombed, a hideous slaughter had been wreaked. For both men – now tired and bedraggled and sated with battle – it was uncomfortable even to think about that. They rode on in silence, drawing steadily away from the city, their horses picking a steady path over a once-fertile, now-trampled plain. Where pomegranate and aubergine had grown in irrigated rows, only char remained; where lines of canes once earmarked the melon and spinach plantations, now there was an immense smouldering refuse.

'Thurstan,' said the boy after a moment, his face pale, streaked with dirt, 'I wanted to drink the sacred waters of Siloam.'

'I know.'

'I wanted to walk the pavements laid by Hadrianus.'

For a moment, Thurstan made no reply. He didn't want to imagine what was happening on those ornate footways now ... two days after the fighting had finished. Both of them could still hear the smashing of furniture and rending of cloth, the shrieks of rapine and carnage, the riotous drunken laughter, the sickening chunk of axe-blade in skull as another wailing mullah was pulled out from hiding.

'Warfare is Hell, lad,' the knight finally said. 'Wherever it occurs.'

'But Thurstan ... there were very few of them soldiers.'

'There were soldiers enough.'

The knight could vividly picture the sky filled with blazing arrows as siege-engines crowded against the walls, the streams of burning pitch from the high stone towers, then the wild melees on the ramparts and down in the passages between the leaning clay tenements ... the screams and curses and slashing blades. Oh ... there'd been soldiers. Of course, in the way of all Infidel armies, those soldiers had fought virtually to the last man, yet when that last man had fallen the furied assault had gone on unabated.

And we thought them barbarians, Thurstan considered.

'They weren't even all of them Saracens,' said Wulfric. 'I saw Jews, Greeks ...'

'Impossible to tell,' the knight replied curtly. In the red mist of his memory, his sweeping long sword clove a variety of faces, yet all were nut-brown, hook-nosed, thickly-bearded. There were no racial differences in this God-forsaken region ... he hoped. 'Especially in the heat of battle.'

'Or massacre,' said the boy.

'Enough talking,' Thurstan replied. 'It won't help to brood. What we're doing now is good.'

Up ahead, beside a natural water-course and a clump of spiny cactus, a small troop of men waited. Some were mounted, some on foot, though like Wulfric and Thurstan, all were girt in slashed, bloody hauberks or thick leather harness now rent and dusty. Many had cast off their helms, loosing lank mats of sweaty hair, or had ripped the cloth crosses from the shoulders of their smoke-grimed cloaks. What few banners they bore trailed the barren ground or hung in shreds. So dirty and dejected were the men, it was impossible to tell knight from serjeant-at-arms, banneret from bowman. As the newcomers arrived, a silent passage appeared among the group, and Reynald la Hors, Knight-Commander of Cerne, was revealed, seated by the water, head-bowed. Wulfric dismounted and hurried forward to embrace him. 'Reynald ... thank God!'

The knight jumped up however, glaring. His eyes were red-rimmed and sore, his once handsome face ingrained with dirt. A deep, clotted sword-cut was visible across the bridge of his nose. 'For Christ's sake, boy,' he snarled. 'In front of the entire house?'

The squire halted in his tracks. 'I ... I thought you were dead.'

Reynald spat out gritty phlegm. 'Do you have anything to drink?'

Unsteadily, shocked, Wulfric turned to his horse and unhooked the wine-skin. 'It's poor quality ...'

'Don't give me some damned trade patter,' the knight-commander grunted, snatching and uncorking it 'Just the drink.'

The boy stood awkwardly as his lord and tutor gulped down the tepid fluid. The others had already lost interest. They sat or stood in silence, fidgeting with weapons, staring at nothing. Only Thurstan watched Reynald, his rugged brown face more sullen than usual.

Wulfric glanced out into the surrounding wilderness. Heat wavered on its dry, dusty ridges. 'They say this land was once a forest, but that the Romans cut down all its trees to make crosses.' He looked back at Reynald. 'Quite appropriate for us, don't you think?'

Reynald wiped his mouth. 'I can't see how that has any relevance at all.'

The squire shook his head, bewildered at the change which had overtaken this once noblest chevalier. 'Then ... why are you here?'

Reynald stared at the boy. 'Why are you here?' he asked. 'You're young, virile. Why aren't you back there?' He indicated the distant, smoggy haze of Jerusalem. 'Using this?' And without warning, he slammed his mailed fist into Wulfric's groin, felling him like a young ox. 'You're landless, nameless ... for God's sake, why aren't you plundering, grabbing your share?'

'You know why,' the boy choked, rolling in agony.

'Damn right!' Reynald snapped, turning away. 'And more fool us.' He spotted Thurstan gazing sourly down at him. 'Do you have a problem, sir?'

'Do you, Reynald?' Thurstan replied. 'Because I think I can resolve it for you.'

Reynald's hand stole to the hilt of his longsword. 'Any time you feel appropriate.'

Thurstan nodded, then slipped down from his saddle. With a rasp of steel, he drew his own blade. They circled each other warily for a moment, then advanced ...

'Enough of this ... in the name of Christ!' cried an angry voice, and Bernard d'Etoille stamped between them.

He was an elderly man, once dignified but now as haggard and dingy as the rest. Arch-Deacon of Salisbury, he'd been advocating this 'holy war' since long before Pope Urban preached it at Clermont four years ago. Even now, his purple robes hung over a suit of chain; the blessed mace he carried, they'd all been caked in Saracen brains. As with so many of them, however, things had rapidly changed for Bernard d'Etoille.

'Hasn't there been enough killing?' he shouted. 'You call yourselves soldiers of Christ, yet after slaughter and theft on a monstrous scale, you're ready for it again ... even in the midst of your penance.'

'Our penance, yes,' said Reynald with a slow smile. 'Now there's a sore point, father-confessor. Who exactly chose this ... penance?'

'Me,' came a deep and resonant voice.

The entire company turned. Almost silently, three more riders had approached. They too were wind-blown and battle-scarred, and despite the searing heat, heavily mailed. One by one, they removed their helms, shaking loose their sodden locks. The central rider, massive in shoulder and a head taller than the other two – in fact, with the exception of Thurstan, a head taller than any man there – was Sihtric fitzOslac, Count of Cerne, Leopard of Gerberoi. He'd always been a stark, imposing man, even dusty and bloodied as he was now. His hair and beard were thick and dark, yet shot with silver, his eyes a piercing blue. There might have been an honest nobility about him, had somebody not once slashed his face to bloody ribbons. Now it was a criss-crossing puzzle of hard, white scars, lending him a near-daemonic countenance.

One after another, his mesnie knelt in deference.

He surveyed them in momentary silence. The duo with him also held their peace, awaiting instruction. The first of these was Joubert, the baron's son – a surly, scowling individual; the second was Simon Navarre, the baron's personal bodyguard. He was Aquitainian by origin, with a thick, guttural accent and feral, dog-like features.

'Do we have a full complement?' the Leopard asked at length.

His warriors rose slowly to their tired feet.

'To some extent, my lord,' said d'Etoille.

'To some extent?' the Leopard replied, staring at him. Unable to explain, the priest looked helplessly down. 'Thurstan?' the baron asked.

Thurstan sniffed. 'Gilbert and Tancred are dead, my lord. Gaillard ... refused to come.'

The baron's mutilated face remained as inscrutable as ever. 'Refused? But I gave orders.'

Thurstan shrugged. 'He was a man possessed when I last saw him, drunk, drenched in blood ... ravishing the harem-girls as if there was no tomorrow.'

'There won't be a tomorrow for him!' snarled Joubert. 'When we return.'

Reynald couldn't resist an ironic chuckle. 'Return?'

The Leopard turned and looked hard at his captain. 'Your faith in me weakens by the day, Reynald.'

'We weaken by the day,' Reynald replied boldly. He gazed out into the grey, smouldering emptiness, into the great haze of heat and sand and shattered rock. 'And now this.'

The Leopard gazed out as well, and couldn't repress a thin smile. 'Yes. This ...'

The Leopard of Gerberoi had a vision, and that vision was Eden ... not some nebulous notion of paradise, some vague province of tranquillity, but the Eden. The very place; that oasis of life in the sun-burned Hell that was this 'Holy Land', this scorched stripe of wilderness on the outer verge of the vast Seljuk Empire. Only there, he'd proclaimed, in the verdant vales where God Himself had stridden and conversed face-to-face with his earliest, most sinless creatures, could they find succour for the heinous crimes of the past three years. Perhaps the Tree of Knowledge would provide answers? Mayhap the Risen Christ, offering gentle palms and tears of joy, waited in its cool shade, eager to reward their effort with lasting forgiveness?

Of course, they'd all been promised similar in those heady, far-off days, when they'd sailed the English Sea and rallied to Duke Robert's standard, to hear the beseeching prayers of Pope Urban's legates. The enthusing cries had gone up and up like birds into the great vaults of the cathedral: 'Any Christian soul, be he ne'er so base, who lifts his spear in the face of the foe, will stake his place in the Heavenly fold no matter the sin he later commits. He who dies fighting in the Lord's name will claim the life eternal on the moment of his departure! Better yet, he who survives the ordeal may seize what he will from the heathen, in direct and lawful reward for the glory of his conquest! God is generous to those who carry his pennon. Destroy the Mohammedan scum. At them! Mind and body! Kill them ... kill them all!'

That wondrous day in Rouen, in the mellow October sunshine, with heraldic banners billowing and a thousand valorous voices cheering, seemed a world away now ... beyond the rivers of blood and bowel shed so savagely at

Dorylaeum and Antioch, beyond the baking wastes of Malabrunias, where Christians had perished in their thousands, riddled with famine, thirst, disease, beyond the towns of Banias and Ma'arra, ravaged and left in seas of avenging flame, their innocent inhabitants scattered and slain like dogs, beyond the flies and the dirt and the sweat and the pain ... and of course, beyond the jabbing blade of guilt, for there were few, in truth, who by the end of the great 'crusade', felt honestly and truthfully that this was the will of the Lord.

Eden ... only Eden, with its tender flowers and fresh-fallen dew, was fit to scour the memory of such calamities. Yet no-one, even d'Etoille, who'd passed his holy tests at Cluny, the home of ascetic leaning, knew for certain where this fabled garden lay, except that it was somewhere to the south-east, beyond Mount Hebron and the Dead Sea. If the thought of this further pilgrimage – now in some vast, trackless land abounding with the sons and brothers of those they'd defiled and slain – filled them with dread, the warrior-priest had already advised those retainers who would listen, that death in their present unclean state would be worse still. In any case, who'd have expected them to cover the immense distance to Jerusalem and survive? Yet they had. And Eden couldn't be so far as that.

First of all, they would seek Uruk ... the earliest city known to Man, built by the banished tribe of Adam, aeons even before the founding-stones were laid at Babylon. A place, it was said, where the first human words were uttered, the first letters written, the first metals struck from the forge. Here, and only here, would they find the maps and scrolls to lead them.

They were perhaps forty in total, straggling in linear formation through the desert of broken stones and scrub-thorn. Wulfric rode on the point, with Thurstan and Reynald. For the most part, they picked their weary way in silence, coated in dust, broiling in their sweat-soaked mail. Every so often, cruel laughter would come up from behind, and the boy would glance back and spy the baron and his son, and their lackey, Navarre, draining their plentiful wineskins, always, it seemed, untroubled.

Wulfric spat froth and mopped his brow. He turned back to the front. They'd been riding five days since Jerusalem, and he was saddle-sore beyond description. His face had thinned to bones, and was wizened as if by age. His long yellow hair lay in plastered streaks on his back, bleached to near-silver. 'Do you gentlemen think those three behind us are truly here for the good of their souls?' he wondered.

'I don't presume to think about my overlord at all,' said Reynald, staring directly ahead. 'Except as knight and master, whose will is beyond question.'

'With all respect, that is a lie,' the boy replied.

Reynald snorted. 'Believe what you will. In the mean time, return to the luggage ... bring me some fruit. My gums are blistering.'

Wulfric gave him a sullen look, then wheeled his horse about and trotted back along the column.

'He's your squire, yet you treat him like a slave,' Thurstan observed.

Reynald shrugged. 'He's English, isn't he. What other way is there?'

Thurstan chuckled. 'A thing I've always wondered about, Reynald ... why a good scion of Tancarville, whose father and brothers charged the English shield-wall at Hastings, then aided the Bastard in all his northern butcheries, should take an English soke-lad and train him for the merit?'

'It's the youngest son's prerogative to behave irrationally, Thurstan. Without a penny to my name, nor a rood of land, it's my belief I can do more or less as I please without having to answer for it.'

Thurstan gave a wry grin. 'Have you always had this secret soft heart?'

Reynald glanced sidelong at him. 'Are you questioning my courage?'

'Not at all ... at Dorylaeum, I saw you break lances with twenty or more Turkish horsemen, and kill at least that number on foot. It was most impressive.'

Reynald said nothing for a moment, then: 'Courage doesn't necessarily translate to cruelty.'

Now Thurstan laughed. 'Splendour of God ... you're even sounding like an Englishman.'

'It's my home, isn't it. I was born there.'

'Norman blood flows in your veins, my friend. It'll take more than a few jugs of Wessex cider to wash it away.'

Reynald shook his head darkly. 'Let me tell you something, Thurstan ... when I joined the Leopard's household at Cerne, it was the greatest moment of my life. My errant days were over. At last I had a roof over my head, a future. Now I could ride in the tourney as part of a company; now my devices were a source of pride rather than indifference. Yet, in my first week, at the request of the drunken scoundrel who was Abbot of Glastonbury, we forced entry to the chapter-house there and slaughtered all the monks who refused to accept his rule. We slaughtered them, Thurstan ... unarmed monks, ten or more. Purely to salve one man's pride.'

'And like Saul to Paul, you were instantly converted.'

'It's a pity you can mock so great a saint,' Reynald replied. 'Especially now that our souls are in peril.'

Thurstan gave a casual smile. 'As household champion, my soul is always in peril. It's a state I've come to live with.'

Reynald shook his head. 'Household champion? You mean protector of the robber's horde. Cerne Castle is a fine place, is it not? Yet the tapestries and hangings which deck its halls once hung in Earl Ethred's long-house. The fine garb, the precious vessels, the heaped silver plate, was the property of his lady ... whose raped carcass, incidentally, adorned a gallows for seven years. Then of course there are the fishponds and ploughland in his former demesnes, the orchards and deer-chase, the flocks and herds ... seized from common-folk whose only weapons were sticks and stones and maybe a thatching-knife.'

'Seized by right of arms.'

'From people who, equally by right of arms, are now refused their liberty as well. Enclosed as villeins on the great manor-estates, denied even tenancy-rights.'

Thurstan shrugged. 'The king's law is our guiding light.'

'And yet we came East?'

'To be shriven.'

'Aye, to be shriven of the king's law.'

Thurstan chuckled again. 'You surprise me, Reynald. You're quite the philosopher. So how do you perceive us now, after Jerusalem?'

'Now?' Reynald gazed ahead – the distant line of the horizon was blurred with oily mist. 'Devils all ... riding back to Tartarus. We seek Eden, but if Adam and Eve were still there, no doubt we'd rob and kill them too.'

Just then, as they spoke, a plume of dust rose up about sixty yards to the front of them ... not wind-borne dust, but soft earth, kicked or back-heeled.

'Did you see that?' said Reynald quietly.

'I did,' Thurstan replied.

Reynald glanced left to right. 'I don't like this ground. It's uneven.'

Thurstan gripped the hilt of his longsword. 'Flanking guard, I think.'

Reynald nodded and turned quickly back to the baron, signalling with his hand. The baron saw him and broke off conversation instantly. Within moments, the word was passing back through the ranks. In less than a minute, the attack came ... but the hardened war-band was already expecting it.

First off, a shoal of arrows rattled down upon them, but they'd ridden out into spear-head formation, Thurstan at the tip, and bore through it with ease, their thick hauberks and heavy limewood shields invulnerable to the light Turkish missiles. Then the ground assault came, a wave of ghostly howls blowing across the desert like wind as the Saracen companies rose up from the surrounding brush, several hundred at least, their horses and camels running neck and neck, the sun glinting on their crescent scimitars, arrows still flying from their double-curved bows.

Wulfric was at the rear, but as always he found battle a terrifying experience. The angry shrieks of his comrades filled him with dread. He cringed with every thwack of arrow on shield or buckler. Sweat ran in rivulets down his face, the confines of his steel helmet baking like an oven tin. He only had a clear view of the Moslems moments before the two forces collided. Apart from their mail shirts and spiked helms, which shone silver in the haze, they were clad all over in black. Cloth obscured even their lower faces, so that all but their frenzied eyes were hidden.

For all that, they were only men. The heavier-armed Christians crashed through their first rank with an explosion of sparks and splinters. Saracen mares reared – blood spurting in fountains from their flaring nostrils, their riders cart-wheeling to earth, transfixed on spear-point or gashed to the brain by axe and sword. Their horsemen behind charged bravely in, but they too were vanquished, struck from the saddle, slashed to pieces as they rode. The fight was far from over of course. Wave after wave of Turkish foot now came forwards in the wake of their cavalry, but the men-at-arms in the baron's company reined up sharply and drove crossbow bolts at them, while the knights galloped gamely into their midst, blades rising and falling in shimmering crimson patterns.

It wasn't all glorious triumph for the crusaders. Wulfric saw several knights unhorsed. One of them was then cut across the throat, and as he toppled onto his back, clawing at the livid wound, a tasselled javelin pinned him to the ground. Even as the squire watched this, a sweeping scimitar struck blood from his own cheek. He spun around in the saddle, trying to rip his sword from its scabbard, and in his efforts to do so, tipped over and fell. The next thing he knew, he was prone ... a Seljuk lancer bearing mercilessly down, only for Thurstan to sweep in from nowhere and intercept, despatching the Turk with a sword-stroke to the skull. A moment later, a Saracen footman came at the boy, screaming. He had already been wounded, for his black pantaloons were slick with gore, and though he aimed a wild blow with his flail, Wulfric was able to parry, then swipe furiously down and hack the man's knees from under him.

All order and formation had now disintegrated, but the ferocious Christian charge, as had happened so frequently in this war, was overwhelming to the lighter-armed Arab forces, ploughing deeply into them, inflicting an instant and fatal wound to their morale. Though the struggle spread in all directions, men scrambling through rocks and scrub, riderless horses careering out of control, far more Moslems had fallen than Christians. Their dead and injured littered the ground in a ghastly flotsam, and those still able to fight were in slow retreat.

Wulfric saw Reynald take a spear in his shield, then with a single backhand slice, lop off the head of the Turk who'd thrust it. Nearby, the baron was felling them left and right, striking out with great butchering blows, his mail glittering with their blood. Navarre had been unhorsed, but chopped his way through a phalanx of foes. When his sword broke, he battled on by hand, seizing a Saracen by the head and twisting sharply, snapping the man's neck like a branch, laughing like a hyena as he did …

In the end, the ambushers left leaving ninety-four behind, some sixty of these dead, the rest grievously wounded. Among the Christians, there were eight fatalities, though this was eight too many for the Leopard of Gerberoi. His vengeance began as darkness fell and camp-fires blazed into the velvet night. The first four prisoners were stripped, then pegged out on the ground, arms and legs splayed … in which position, Navarre and his minions proceeded to push clods of earth into their frothing mouths, forcing them down their gullets with sticks or knives.

'Pack them full!' said Joubert with a laugh. 'They can eat this whole country if they want – earth, rocks, roots, the lot. We'll stuff them 'til their bellies burst, but we'll have words out of them.'

Wulfric went sick at the sight, and had to turn away and clap his hands over his ears to drown out the retching, the gagging, the rattling gasps for air. Arch-Deacon d'Etoille refused outright to be party to it. Earlier that day, he'd fought as bravely as the rest, but this, he said, was a cruelty he could scarce believe. The Leopard had smiled at that, then given orders for the torture to commence. The rest of the company, cut, bruised and tired from the fight, now watched in brooding silence, though at length Reynald turned to Thurstan. 'You think this will avail us anything at all?' he wondered.

The household champion shrugged. 'Depends what they know. We've fought Arabs of every tribe … Seljuks, Fatamids. But there are some among these I've never seen before … the ones in black. We need to know who they are, at least.'

Reynald shook his head. 'There'll be an answer for it. There always is.'

Initially that answer was a positive one, for one of those captives not yet put to the test, finally fell on his knees, begging mercy of the baron.

'Bismil lah atlubukal rahma,' he jabbered, eyes bulging like black jewels in his bearded, wood-brown face. 'Atlubuka hayati wasawfa akoolo lak ma tawoodu an ta'arif.'

Navarre strode forward. Before he'd come to the Anglo-Norman camp during the Scottish war, the surly Aquitainian had served many times as mercenary with the armies of Aragon and Castille in their ceaseless strife with the Moors. In result, he had more than a smattering of Arabic, and now grinned broadly as he wiped his bloody hands on a piece of rag. 'He wants to make a bargain with us, my lord.'

The Leopard gazed down at the cowering captive. 'Ask him who sent them?'

Navarre did so, and their prisoner spoke eagerly, though many times he glanced over his shoulder as if in fear of his former comrades, who were still bound but listening intently. When he had finished, even Navarre was briefly silent. 'They are Ashishin,' the knight finally said. 'Sent by Hasan bin Sabah, the "Old Man of the Mountain".'

'You know them?' asked the Leopard.

Navarre nodded. 'I've heard of them. But I thought them myth. They're a Persian sect by origin, and fanatics. Totally dedicated to serving their master. He is a prophet and, by rumour, a sorcerer. He lives purely to destroy the enemies of Islam. Even the caliphs of Bagdhad, whom he has called heretics, fear his influence ... so Salib-een, like us, are particularly loathed.' The Aquitainian considered. 'These are truly dangerous men, my lord.'

The Leopard's only response was to smile, then to slowly draw his hunting-knife. He turned to their prisoner. 'Not this one.'

Again, the Turk fell onto his face, weeping and pleading aloud. 'Arjook la taqtalani!'

'He still wishes to talk,' said Navarre.

'Does he know of Uruk?' the baron asked.

Navarre relayed the question, and though the captive at first seemed surprised, he was soon nodding eagerly, babbling a response.

The Aquitainian grinned. 'He says it lies to the east ... in ruins. But he also says we might find treasure there, if we search hard enough.'

At this, Arch-Deacon d'Etoille interceded. 'Treasure is not our quest ... my lord?'

Ignoring the priest, the Leopard placed a foot on his prisoner's shoulder and stared down at him. 'Tell him ... tell him that if he can lead us to Uruk, his life is spared.'

Navarre passed the message on, and the Turk rolled his eyes in glee, planting kisses on the baron's boot. 'Ashluruka ya sayiddi lihikmatika wa rahmatika.'

'He will do as we ask,' said Navarre.

'Good.' The baron kicked the man away. 'But kill the rest. We've no use for them.'

'Lord Sihtric!' d'Etoille cried. 'You have them in your grasp. They are no threat to you.'

The baron laughed. 'Until they clamour for shares in our food and drink.'

'Can't you release them disarmed?'.

'When they've overheard this conversation? Out of the question!' And the Leopard strode away.

A moment later there was a succession of thuds and gasps, as heavy blades ripped into heaving breastbones. The Turk who had betrayed his friends could only kneel and watch, red phantoms of firelight playing over him.

D'Etoille lurched off to hide, though Thurstan briefly stopped him. 'I wouldn't despair too much, Father,' said the champion. 'Didn't we christen the Lord's own lance, when we found it at Antioch, by plunging it through the entrails of every heathen dog we came to?'

The cleric gave him a haunted, horrified look before staggering away into the darkness.

'Anyone would think you approved,' Reynald remarked.

'All I approve of at the moment, my friend, is my own survival.' Thurstan peered beyond the lights of the paltry camp, and for the first time, saw strange and amorphous things in the swollen night. 'But I think we finally agree on something ... there'll be answers had for this.'

For another week they pressed on, though now through a blighted wilderness, a blasted empty terrain, bare of water or vegetation, yet strewn – bizarrely – with boulders of colossal size. Their scout and apparent new friend, whose name was Hasif, told them Uruk was still a regal place of colonnades, statues and fabulous temples, but that it stood on a spur of land between the rivers Tigris and Euphrates, and to reach it they must first cross the burned waste of Arabia's northern desert. This would be an arduous journey of a week or more, in the fiercest heat imaginable. To illustrate his point, the guide bound his hands and face with strips of cloth, so that he looked like a bedouin, and advised his captors to do the same.

'This is blasphemy,' said Reynald, as they decked themselves.

Thurstan chuckled. 'To adapt to barbaric conditions, Reynald, we must first become barbaric men.'

'More so than we already are? That would be a miraculous feat.'

Wulfric made no comment. Before them now lay an empty vista of sand, occasional flurries billowing up like ghosts. There were also insects – huge, black, stinging things, which clustered on the horses and swarmed around the men, adding torment to torment. The boy wasn't sure if he could take much more. He'd drunk his water-ration not five minutes before, yet his mouth was already dry as shale. The sun was a suspended furnace, occupying most of the sky ... it was impossible even to glance at it. There was grit in Wulfric's eyes, salt in his cracked lips, a deep weariness in his bones. All of a sudden, the cool English greenwood, with its carpet of mist and scent of earth and rain, was as unreal to him as Jerusalem had been when he was back in Wessex. In those days, the Holy City had seemed the furthest destination possible, and indeed years had passed in the getting there, yet everything the boy knew, including that now-desecrated shrine, lay uncountable leagues behind him. What lay to his front was anyone's guess.

Or maybe, anyone's nightmare.

The true ordeal began a day later. They'd pitched their animal-hide tents on a barren wadi, but arose from them early ... to find their three piquets missing. At first there was an assumption the men had frozen and now lay buried in the drifting sand, but quick searches revealed no trace.

'Ashishin?' Reynald wondered, as they stood there in bewilderment.

The baron looked to Navarre, who slammed a fist into the guts of their prisoner and demanded an explanation.

'Ma'ariffi la ya'khidoon asra,' the Saracen gasped, as he writhed in the dust.

Navarre stepped back. 'He says the Ashishin take no prisoners. And they'd have left the bodies here, to frighten us.'

The Leopard of Gerberoi gazed out across the rolling desert. Again, nothing was visible, except swirling eddies of sand. The only sound was a faint hiss of the wind. Infinitesimally, the baron's eyes narrowed, and for the first time Wulfric wondered if he saw foreboding there, maybe even fear? Was such a thing possible? Had this brute warrior, this iron-fisted man-bear, who'd served two kings with such ferocity, and at Gerberoi slew so many rebel knights with his scything longsword that the jongleurs had named him for it, finally found something which frightened him?

'Their horses are still here,' said Thurstan, coming back from the corral. 'So they haven't deserted. Tonight we'll post a fuller watch.'

The baron nodded.

That night too, however, there were disasters. Six sentries were posted, yet all had vanished by dawn. What was worse, the sand lay smooth around their posts, like fresh-fallen snow. Had any one of them fled on foot, or been approached through the dark, either by murderous man or predatory beast, the tracks would have been clearly visible. In the space of a few days, the company was down to twenty-three; almost half the number they'd struck out with from Jerusalem, less than a third of those who'd originally departed Cerne.

A silent dread now went through them all, though for Wulfric it went further still ... for during the past two nights he'd suffered the same frightful dream. In it, he'd lain senseless on an arid plain, too weak to move. The sky had been filled with circling vultures, but on all sides of him statues of cyclopean stone had lowered – titanic effigies of kings and popes. So vast were they, that their grim, tyrannical features completely filled his vision, yet in that way of all dream-selves, he had seen much more than this; a living being was also present, a quick-darting thing of vaguely human shape. It had first appeared some distance away, scurrying here and there, peeping about between the statues' gargantuan feet, but now drawing closer to him.

Of course the boy never mentioned this. At the end of the day, a dream was only a dream. On the third night, however, went eight men were despatched to sentry, he was stricken with indecision. If this group was lost too, and he'd sounded no alarum, didn't that make it his fault? He bedded down in his master's tent, bundled in hides, his mind filled with doubts. Their entire world seemed to be collapsing: scarcely a word was spoken amongst the company any more, their food-stocks were down to rinds of bread and withered citrus fruit, their water almost spent. He himself, unconsciously, was neglecting his squire's duties – his tending to horse, apparel, weaponry – yet Reynald was too disinterested to upbraid him.

And so thinking, the boy drifted again into his dreams, where as before, the darting, peeping thing awaited, though now it had approached to a distance of several yards and was stealthily creeping closer. In his slumber, Wulfric tried to shout, for he suddenly had a horror of this thing, which even as he lay there, he could now see in all its grisly glory: Manlike, yes, almost, but with dark and gleaming skin and a face of fantastic malevolence: crocodile teeth gleamed between lips curved in a manic grin; oriental eyes flashed cruelty beneath a heavy brocade of blue Moorish shadow; pearls glistened in its ears; its hair was black as oil and hung in slick, perfumed knots. And as it reached down towards him, he saw the nails on its fingers; they were sharp and twisting, like talons …

Wulfric woke, thinking he was shrieking aloud, but really with only a whimper trapped in his throat.

Gasping, wet with sweat, he scrambled out from the tent into the silent camp. The stillness out there was awesome. To all sides, the desert lay vast and empty – again, it reminded him of snow-shrouded December morns in England, though now strawberry streaks of dawn filled the sky and the icy chill was rapidly diminishing. Shivering, stretching his cramped limbs, the squire walked hurriedly back and forth. Already the horror of the dream was fading, though its memory remained vivid. Had the thing screamed at him as well?, he wondered. Hadn't he just heard some ghastly falsetto screech?

The boy stopped in his tracks.

He looked slowly out beyond the tents again … the sentries were absent.

Hardly daring to breathe, the squire ventured to the boundary, where stones and spears had been set in a makeshift palisade. Nobody patrolled it. He glanced left to right … there was no mistake. The eight guards posted the night before were definitely missing. He gazed once more at the shifting dunes, half expecting to see that peeping, darting form. Still there was nothing ... only twists of billowing sand. And then a hand clamped his shoulder ... a heavy, calloused hand. Wulfric whirled around.

Joubert was standing there, his face dark with hatred. 'FitzUrz,' he said slowly. 'I might've guessed an English pig would be at the root of this. Stealing out again to murder our people?'

Wulfric gazed blankly at the baron's son, momentarily perplexed. He had no idea why, but Joubert had been an enemy of his from the moment he'd arrived at Cerne as a stable-lad. In fact, he'd long ago given up wondering about it. The young nobleman was simply a boor, he'd decided ... strong, thick of limb, barrel of body, but renownedly arrogant, cold and treacherous.

'I ... I couldn't sleep, my lord,' the boy tried to explain.

'Neither could I,' Joubert replied. 'Which was fortunate ... was it not?'

Wulfric shook his head. 'I'm no murderer.'

Joubert's lip curled. 'Like all English, a coward too.'

And at that, Wulfric – still dazed, still frightened – was finally stung. 'Unlike you Normans, of course,' he retorted, 'who after the fall of King Harold, festooned your gibbets with his wounded carls.'

The baron's son lashed out with the speed of a snake, slapping Wulfric fiercely on the cheek. It was a terrific blow, and the lad was staggered where he stood.

'King Harold was a perjured usurper!' Joubert snarled. 'My father can tell you. He was newly-knighted that day. No older than you. Yet he cut his way with ease to your so-called king.' The Norman chuckled. 'He took the royal bollocks on the tip of his sword.'

Wulfric spat at Joubert's feet. 'Aye ... after the king had already fallen, an arrow-barb buried in his eye!'

Reynald came out from his tent struggling to wake, but his ears filled with grunts, growls, ribald shouts. At first he saw members of the mesnie leaping about excitedly, as if at a cock-fight or ratting pit. For several seconds more, he was too befuddled with sleep to realise exactly what was happening ... then it struck him that two of the men were fighting, wrestling on the ground like drunken peasants. He stepped forward, only half interested ... but was stunned when he saw the flopping yellow mane of Wulfric.

'What the devil!' Angrily, the knight pushed his way through, for a second revelation to strike him: Joubert! Dear God!

For a moment Reynald was in turmoil. This was the way it should be, the way all men – from gallant knights to stinking Brabancons – ought to settle quarrels; head to head on the field of honour. But this was no fair duel.

Joubert might be an insufferable braggart who rated his powers more highly than he should, but he was still a knight, whereas Wulfric was only a squire. Joubert was ruthless enough to go for the kill, because that was the way he had been taught; Wulfric, on the other hand, would balk at inflicting serious injury ... and rightly so, for his opponent was a magnate-in-waiting.

Reynald decided he'd stop this straight away.

But he was just about to move in, when a knife-point pricked the flesh below his ear. He froze ... a brawny arm folded across his throat. Then he heard Navarre's leering voice - the guttural Lange d'Oc thick with scorn. 'Not one step,' the dog chuckled. 'The Leopard's son will have his little diversions.'

'You bastaaaa ...' Reynald began, but a third voice cut him dead.

'You put a blade to the household banneret? You dare! You blasted whoreson!'

Reynald felt the arm relax. He lurched away and turned. Thurstan had appeared, as bleary-eyed as the rest, but now holding a spear to Navarre's neck, its tapering point pressed so firmly against the flesh that droplets of blood had appeared. 'Drop it!'

The Aquitainian held his arms aloft, but refused to relinquish his knife. 'I'm not part of your damned household!' he snarled defiantly, though his voice was wary, his eyes wide with fear.

'Drop it, or I'll spit you like a fish!'

Reluctantly, Navarre released the weapon. Reynald whirled back to Wulfric and Joubert, still going at each other like wild animals, biting, clawing. The squire was giving a reasonable account of himself, though he was the more bloodied of the two; both his lips were burst like ripe plumbs. The knight hauled them apart, kicking Wulfric to one side and dragging Joubert away by the coif, throwing him heavily in the dust. There were groans of disapproval from the spectators. One or two cursed; some even issued threats.

Most outraged, however, was Joubert, who clambered swiftly to his feet, voice cracking in fury. 'You bass cur!' he squealed. 'I'll kill you, kill you ...'

He dived at the nearest man-at-arms, yanked a broadsword from the man's scabbard, then wheeled frenziedly about ... only to be dealt a stunning blow to the jaw by a thickly gloved fist.

A silence fell over the retinue. They gazed in awe at the baron, whose huge right hand was still tightly clenched. He returned their gaze intensely, focusing in particular on Reynald. Fleetingly, the knight saw his overlord as he once had been, when they'd fought together, hunted together, ridden in the tourney as friends ... before the Norse had torn his face apart at Anglesey, before the madness of conquest had grown on him like a fever.

'No-one,' said the baron after a moment, his voice a taut whisper, 'no-one ... dies in this company, without my say-so first.' He kicked his fallen son.

'Up sirrah! Get up!'

Groggily, drooling blood, Joubert raised himself onto all fours. 'I should … should've beaten him to death,' he mumbled.

The baron was unimpressed. 'The progress you were making, we'd have been here all day. Up!' He glanced sideways, to where Thurstan was still holding his spear at Navarre's throat. Their eyes met, and after a moment, Thurstan lowered the weapon. Immediately, Navarre retrieved his knife and whipped around, dragging a gauntlet from his belt. He was clearly about to issue a challenge to Thurstan, when a cry came wavering across the tents towards them. A breathless, haunted cry: 'My Lord! My Looooord!'

Almost as one, they turned. So desperate was the cry, that the entire band thrust its way through the encampment to the southern perimeter, where two visions awaited them. First of all, there was Arch-Deacon d'Etoille. Under the hardships of the last few days, he had degenerated more than most. Once portly, he was now emaciated; tired, wasted flesh hung at his jowls. Once devout, he now knew little for sure … save only that the Crossed Keys of the papal banner were spattered over and over with innocent blood. Even his aggressive intellect had faded … he couldn't reason in a land where reason no longer applied. When they came upon him now, he stood violently shaking, features pale as ice, gazing out into the desert …which was where the second vision awaited them.

Where it had come from, they didn't know; what it was, they had no clue. At first, they were too stunned by it to speak … on every head the hair prickled, on every body the weary flesh crawled.

Perhaps thirty yards away, a body of dust and dirt was spinning at phenomenal speed, as if some spiralling wind had seized it. It was like the central funnel of a dust-storm, only smaller, more compact … upright by fifteen feet, maybe five-feet across. So dense was it, though, that nothing was visible through it. It swirled with frightful force, giving off a rushing, breathless roar.

'What … what in the name of God …' Reynald stammered.

More horror-stricken than anyone else though, was Hasif. With a wailing cry, he sank to his knees, hands clasped. 'Sawfa nahlik jamee'an!'

'What does he say?' the baron demanded. 'Navarre, what does he say?'

It took the Aquitainian several seconds to regain sufficient composure to speak with the man, and when he did, the response he got was broken and tearful. Hasif could only gaze red-eyed and despairing at the apparition. 'Al-iblees khulika minal riyah!' he stuttered. 'La tareeq lil hiroob …'

When Navarre looked back to his overlord, he too had paled. He swallowed before he could speak. 'He says … he says it is djinn, sent for us by the Old Man. A spirit of earth and air, charged with our destruction. It will not cease its pursuit until we are all dead.'

'It's a judgement on us!' d'Etoille cried, reaching under his tattered purple and drawing out an iron crucifix. 'We came here in the name of Christ, and in the name of Christ we slew babes and robbed houses.' He stepped over the line of rocks marking the camp boundary. 'We're brigands,' he wept, 'but the worst kind of brigands ... for we use God's holy will as our excuse.'

'What the devil are you doing?' Thurstan shouted, trying to grab him but missing.

'Lord Jesus!' Arch-Deacon d'Etoille prayed, now advancing out of reach, his crucifix held high. 'I beg you to take into your bosom the soul of this Thine servant, who today dies accursed in a hellish place.'

'My lord!' Navarre hissed. 'We must get away from here.'

He even clutched his overlord's arm, but the baron shook him off, gazing at the spectacle before them in morbid fascination.

'I entreat You,' the priest beseeched, 'deliver me not into the hands of Satan ...'

But his words ended mid-sentence in a shrill and prolonged scream, for without warning, the thing suddenly rushed upon him. The rest of the company watched aghast as he was enveloped. Instantly, he clamped his hands to his face, as if to protect his eyes, but was buffeted back and forth, and a second later, yanked upwards from his feet in horizontal levitation, whence he began to spin and spin at ever greater speed. Within moments he was a purple blur and nothing more, and then ... he was gone; he winked out like a candle-flame.

A moment of stupefied silence followed, the remaining men too mesmerised to react ... before the abomination spat something out, which thudded into the sand close to their feet. They gazed down ... at Father d'Etoille's crucifix, now a twisted knot of melted iron

And at that, they went amok. With wild shrieks, they were suddenly falling over each other to get to the horses. Tents were knocked flat, cooking-pots kicked over, backpacks and weapons left strewn ...

The swirling monstrosity gave no immediate or hurried chase ... almost as if it knew it could bide its time.

If the thing actually had a mind and strategies, then their panic-stricken flight gave it a keen advantage. Supplies had been lost, horses scattered. Many men were separated from the main party, and highly likely the supernatural foe went on to pick these off, for within four hours Wulfric found himself part of a fellowship comprising only himself, Thurstan, Reynald, Joubert, Navarre, the baron and Hasif, and in possession only of the items they'd been wearing or carrying in their bolsters.

Regardless of their missing friends, they continued to ride fast and hard for the remainder of that day, pushing blindly on through bleak, arid emptiness, but now in frantic disorder. When they finally slowed to a walk, breathless and sweating, their horses lathered, there were no words between them. Ordinarily in such circumstances there might have been regret at the reckless haste, shame at the apparent cowardice ... now there were only frightened glances, whispered prayers. They pitched camp in a high, rocky place, but without tents and bedrolls, were mercilessly exposed to the raw desert night. In consequence none of them slept, and when the morning came, they were sorely tired. The temptation was to stay and doze, but common sense forbade it ... if the stalking daemon didn't despatch them, the sun surely would.

'Are we sure this thing is real?' Reynald asked, as they rode on.

'You saw if for yourself,' Thurstan replied.

'I think we've had lotus crushed in our water-stock. Such devils don't exist.'

Thurstan shook his head. 'Pagan lands ... pagan things.'

Reynald turned in his saddle. 'Is it following us?'

'You want to stay to find out?' Navarre wondered. 'You saw what it did to d'Etoille.'

'I saw you leading the charge to get away from it,' Reynald mocked.

The Aquitainian glared round with fresh fury, but the baron interjected. 'Real or not,' he said in a resolute tone, 'we have our penance to perform.'

'We do?' Reynald whispered to Thurstan. Even with the company decimated, the quest apparently went on. 'This is complete folly.'

'Still questioning me, Reynald?'

'Oh ... forgive me, my Lord. I thought that by now we might have paid God His dues.'

'We haven't,' the baron assured him, though once again the great noble glanced over his shoulder, and Wulfric saw further apprehension, uncertainty, maybe even alarm. Of course, opponents of every sort were to be expected in a land like this, though the Leopard of Gerberoi had clearly not expected this one.

The next morning they followed a parched river-bed, and by the height of noon, came across stunted trees, where some modicum of shelter was had. The tan crags of mountains were starting to emerge in the north-east. Wulfric wondered which range it was. It suddenly struck him as ludicrous that not one of them knew where they were any more, and hadn't done for days. They were completely in the hands of a Moslem prisoner, who had every reason to despise them ... though at present Hasif seemed more afraid than devious. When he wasn't riding, he passed the time either cowering on his prayer-mat, or gazing fearfully behind.

The thing he dreaded, the djinn or wind-daemon, or whatever it was, for the moment at least chose to remain hidden, though none of them doubted it was somewhere close at hand. Why it didn't attack was anyone's guess. Wulfric's premonition dreams – for he'd decided this was what they were – had also faded, though in truth he slept only fitfully from this moment on, protected solely by his cloak in the frozen nights and spending the daylight hours in fatigued delirium. A week later, when a fierce sandstorm blew up, he bore through it in drugged, careless fashion. The morning after that, when the baron announced that as their water and bread was now virtually used, they would proceed on quarter-rations, the boy made no comment. He wondered if he was close to death ... and even at that prospect, he felt strangely unconcerned.

Uncountable hours of this torment passed before, suddenly – without any warning – there was grass on the hills again; dry, prickly grass, but still grass. A day later, the travellers were seeing cork oaks, olive trees, even clumps of cedar ... and then, the news came that they were near their goal. Navarre delivered it. As was their way, Wulfric, Thurstan and Reynald were lagging far behind the others, moving only at a snail's pace, when the baron's bodyguard came galloping back towards them.

'Half a day,' he said, reining excitedly up. 'Our Arabic pet assures us. Half a day to the river, and beyond that ... Uruk.' They made no answer, which seemed to displease him. 'You've come this far, you ought at least to be glad we've arrived!'

Thurstan hawked and spat.

'You miserable dogs,' the Aquitainian sneered. 'The wealth of ages awaits us ... the treasure-house of Persia ... gold, silver. Mountains of it, and all you can do is ...' His words tailed off for a moment; he seemed as bewildered as he was sickened. 'To Hell with you all!'

Angrily, he wheeled his horse about and cantered back. The other three plodded on in weary silence, though after a moment Wulfric began to chuckle. 'I always suspected our overlord was only partially a penitent man?'

'What does it matter?' Reynald grunted. 'We swore fealty?'

'We've followed him half way across the world,' the boy replied, his mirth drying up. 'I think we've exercised our fealty.'

'It's not your place to think, Wulfric.'

'No, of course not,' said the squire, 'when there are so many others here thinking for me.' Suddenly he was choking back tears ... or would have been, if there'd been sufficient moisture left in his body. 'We raided Jerusalem in God's name, but there were too many thieves to make it pay; so in the guise of penance, we now raid Uruk.' He shook his head. 'The search for Eden ... I actually believed that!'

'There is no Uruk,' Thurstan put in grimly. 'How could there be? A city older than Babylon? I'd be surprised if one brick stood on another.'

'Then what are we doing here?' the boy protested.

'I'd suggest you go back,' said Reynald. 'I'd even knight you, to make it lawful ... but I don't know which way is back. And then, of course ...' and now it was his turn to chuckle, a crazy fluting sound, 'then of course, our daemonic friend is back there somewhere.'

'I'm scarcely worried about that thing,' the squire snorted. 'It's probably in awe of us, demoralised ... it found out what we did in Jerusalem and realises it can't compete ...'

'Enough ranting!' Thurstan interrupted. 'Enough of it! Just save your breath. You might need it yet.'

Defeated, the boy hung his head and said no more. Neither of the men spoke either. Hours passed as they swayed aimlessly along, the sun a sphere of burnished brass directly above them. Only the crunch and crackle of broken, cinder-dry stones beneath their horses' hooves, could be heard ... that, and the occasional haunting cry of eagle or buzzard. Ahead, the horizon rippled as if oiled and greased by the heat. The baron and his group were ghost-like in it, elongated, cut up into fragments, and then gradually flattened and consumed as they crested some ridge and bore down the other side of it.

And it was then, roughly, that the first silvery chuckles of water made themselves known. The sound alone was refreshing, revitalising.

Wulfric glanced up, his dusty mouth curved in a curious frown. 'Is that ... can that be ...?'

'I think it is,' Reynald muttered. 'God's bread, that dog Navarre was telling the truth!' He urged his horse forwards eagerly.

'Only about the river,' Thurstan cautioned, hanging back.

'The river's enough, isn't it,' Reynald said, breaking into a gallop.

Wulfric followed him, and five minutes later the two of them mounted a low ridge and found themselves gazing down on a wide shallow valley, in the centre of which a river flowed ... an enormous river; the mythical Euphrates, vast and brown and deeply swollen, but gliding mirror-smooth between steep shingle banks.

'Thank you, oh Lord!' the squire loudly prayed.

'Don't ... don't thank Him yet,' said Reynald, in a strained and suddenly tight voice. He pointed down the slope with shaking finger. 'What ... what is that?'

Thurstan, who had now come up behind them, shielded his eyes, then spurred his horse downhill in order to get a closer look. The others went too, but they'd only descended several dozen feet, before the full ghastliness of what they were seeing became clear to them.

Thirty-four wooden poles had been erected in a row on the river's nearest shore, every one at least twelve feet tall. From the top of each was suspended the body of a man. The first nine were battle-field corpses, the men killed in the fight with the Ashishin, now decayed to carrion and thick with dust ... for they'd been removed from their graves. The remaining twenty-seven were more recognisable; Arch-Deacon d'Etoille was among them for example, along with others who'd vanished during the trek across Arabia. These had been more freshly slain, and in most cases more brutally. Torn and ripped, as if by giant claws, they hung in blood-soaked tatters. Bird-pecked entrails were visible, shreds of muscle and sinew; spears of snapped bone jutted out through multiple jagged wounds.

Even after everything they'd seen and done, the three crusaders found this a scene of near-overwhelming horror. Wulfric swooned from his saddle, the gorge rising in his throat; Reynald dismounted and sank to his knees. Thurstan was lost for words ... he closed his eyes, unwilling to acknowledge the vision. Men died in war, that was taken for granted, but not like this ... to be flayed, eviscerated, then displayed like scarecrows! And what about the dead? Dear God, it had even ploughed up the dead! What kind of monster was this?

'Have you ... have you ever known such a thing?' Reynald finally asked, his voice a whisper.

Thurstan clambered down from his saddle, shaking his head. Beyond the grisly exhibits, he now spied the entrance to a bridge; an extremely flimsy bridge, by the looks of it – little more than sticks and rope – but spanning the river to its far shore. Beside it, there was a low granite pillar, to which three horses had been tethered. He cursed bitterly. 'I hoped the wretched thing had taken the baron as well, and his son and their bloody guard-dog ... but I doubt it would've tarried to secure the horses.'

Now Reynald spotted the animals too. For a second he was confused. 'Then ... where are they?'

'Where do you imagine?' Thurstan laughed darkly. 'Beyond this river lies Uruk ... the treasure-house of ancient Persia.'

'What?' Reynald rose unsteadily to his feet, ashen-faced. 'He ... could leave these men like this? His own retainers ... who've followed him half way across the world! He could leave them hanging here, just to find trove!' His voice had risen to an angry shout. 'How could he do that? How?'

Before Thurstan could answer, however, Wulfric interrupted them ... with an hysterical scream: 'IT'S HERE! IT'S COME FOR US!'

The two men spun around ... and went cold. On the top of the slope behind them, the djinn had re-appeared, in all its swirling ferocity, only now it seemed enraged, for it was red and seething, as if dense crimson dust was mingled inside it. With a howl of elemental fury, it swept down the hill towards them. Though it was still a hundred yards away at least, the horses shrieked and bolted. The squire found himself staggering backwards into the midst of the two knights, though both of them were grey-faced with shock at the sight and fury of the monster

'It isn't toying with us any more,' said Thurstan slowly. Then, with sudden determination, he ripped the longsword from his scabbard. 'Over the river with you both … hurry!'

Reynald stared at him in disbelief. 'What … what are you going to do?'

Thurstan grinned broadly. 'My job. As household champion, I must always be first into battle, last out … must I not?'

'Are you mad?'

'Remember Nicaea, Reynald … our rearguard held the sultan at bay for a whole day.' Thurstan drew his dagger as well. 'The siege-lines held … remember? The Turks were completely broken.'

'But this is a spirit, a devil!'

Blades levelled, Thurstan began to advance. 'Away with you now …don't make my last glorious gesture a futile one.'

Reynald gazed dumbly after him, then turned to the squire, who waxy-white though he was, could only shake his head. 'We … we can't leave him, Reynald.'

The knight grabbed the boy by the shoulder and thrust him towards the bridge. 'We must!'

Thurstan had ridden countless jousts, fought many a duel to the death in the name of his overlord … land and tenure disputes, impeachment, trial-by-battle. But never had he met a foe like this. It roared and growled and spat out broken rocks as it thundered towards him. Since he had last seen it, it had grown to immense proportions, expanding its height to thirty feet at least, its girth to fifteen. Even then, the sight of the fearless warrior approaching seemed baffling to it. Its livid hues temporarily faded, the frenzied headlong charge appeared to falter. Instead of coming mindlessly on, it slowed, shifting sideways as if circling … sizing him up before it attacked.

Thurstan gave a great belly-laugh. He hefted his sword. 'You don't fancy this, hey? Maybe cold steel can hurt you after all.' The knight pulled up his coif, then sank to a crouch. The muscles bunched in his powerful legs. 'They call my people 'the sword-bearers of Christ'!' he shouted. 'We fear no-one … Danes, Bretons, English, Franks. We've beaten them all! '

With an earth-shaking rumble, the daemon surged towards him. Thurstan sprang to meet it …

*

The bridge over the Euphrates was a perilous thing to cross. It was so narrow that only one man could pass over it at a time. More worrying still, its planking had rotted in many places, while the hemp ropes were loose and frayed. The entire structure swung and creaked as they picked their way across. The river-surface was only ten feet below, but it clearly ran deep and both Reynald and Wulfric still wore mail beneath their leather. To make things worse, they were only half way across when a figure appeared at the far end, blocking their path. Reynald stopped in his tracks, watching as the figure then advanced onto the bridge.

'Who is that?' said Wulfric from behind.

'Navarre,' Reynald replied after a second. 'And for some reason … his blade is drawn.' He didn't need to turn and look, to know that the safety of the western bank was a long way behind them. With a low sigh, the knight loosed the strap on his sword-hilt. 'Remind me, Wulfric,' he said, 'if we ever get back to civilisation, that I am too old for stupid, foolish games like this!'

He proceeded, the boy following, but they'd only covered two thirds of the bridge before Navarre stopped them. He now stood directly in front, and grinned ghoulishly, the teeth very white in his bristling, dog-like race. 'Lord Sihtric, Count of Cerne … charges me with defending this position,' he said. 'I am obliged to follow that order until further notice. Henceforth, none shall pass.'

'Don't be an imbecile,' Reynald snapped. 'Stand aside.'

'None shall pass!' Navarre reiterated, now hefting his longsword. After so much battle, it was notched and scarred, but it still had a keen edge. More to the point, of course, the man wielding it was notoriously an expert … only Thurstan, it was said, could match him, and that would be more through brute strength than genuine skill.

Reluctantly, Reynald drew his own sword. 'I will tell you one more time, Aquitaine … I am Knight-Commander of Cerne, and you must step aside.'

Navarre's response was an amused grin, a shake of his head, then a furious chestward lunge …

The baron and his son found Uruk all they had dreamed of, and more. The moment they stepped out from the narrow gully in the low hillside, they were there … in the heart of ancient Sumer, the most celebrated citadel in all antiquity lying empty and open before them.

Hasif forgotten, Navarre forgotten, all else forgotten, they'd staggered breathlessly forward and now were wandering dazed among monuments of a size and grandeur neither Rome nor Athens had ever dreamed of. Much of what they saw was green with age, cracked, overgrown by vines and brambles, yet still it bespoke the pomp and richness of a lost heroic era. On all sides, gargantuan columns – cut from onyx or marble, veined with quartz – soared to portico roofs. Triumphal arches led through to vast squares and amphitheatres floored with intricate mosaics. There were statues of shimmering bronze, ornate friezes, temples adorned with ancient symbols, arcane glyphs.

Neither of the Norman warlords was overly entranced by this, of course. They were hard men, cold men, whose court was the military camp. They had no real taste for things they had never known, like beauty, luxury. Wealth, on the other hand ... wealth was a different matter. Eagerly, they sought it out.

Blow for blow, they battled on the rope-bridge. It was as precarious a fight as Reynald had ever fought. Navarre struck with savage, swiping blows, which the Norman needed every ounce of his strength to parry or evade. His own counter-attack, vigorous and repeated, was deflected with ease, and already blood streamed from fresh slashes on his face and hands. His bone-weary legs were quivering beneath him.

The longswords clashed and clashed, the combatants grunted, the ropes and timbers squealed and hummed. Wulfric could only encourage his master. The narrow passage prevented him coming alongside to help, and in any case, such a thing would have been dishonourable. Not that he cared about that now. His lord, he saw, was exhausted, mouth agape, face running with sweat. Again Navarre caught the Norman, this time across the belly, the ripping sword-point laying bare the felt beneath the mail. On this occasion, though, Reynald responded well, with a hefty thrust to the Aquitainian's throat, causing him to grimace and draw back a step ... and then to overbalance. Navarre grabbed wildly at the support-ropes, briefly leaving himself unguarded, allowing Reynald to thrust again. This attack caught Navarre on the shoulder, but was insufficient to punch through the chain and leather padding. Enraged, the baron's man fought back, aiming stroke after stroke at Reynald's head. The aged timbers cracked and splintered beneath their stamping, skidding feet.

Wulfric found he was clinging on for dear life as the bridge swung and tilted. He needed to act, he realised, or they'd all be drowned ... and his moment came sooner than he'd expected, for with a chilling crunch, part of the footing suddenly gave, the timbers under Reynald breaking away entirely. Desperately, the Norman flung himself to one side, trusting his entire weight to the support-rope. The Aquitainian leaped after him, slamming an elbow into his throat, forcing him back further. Reynald gagged. He chopped downwards with his sword, but Navarre, now chest-to-chest, was too close for it to

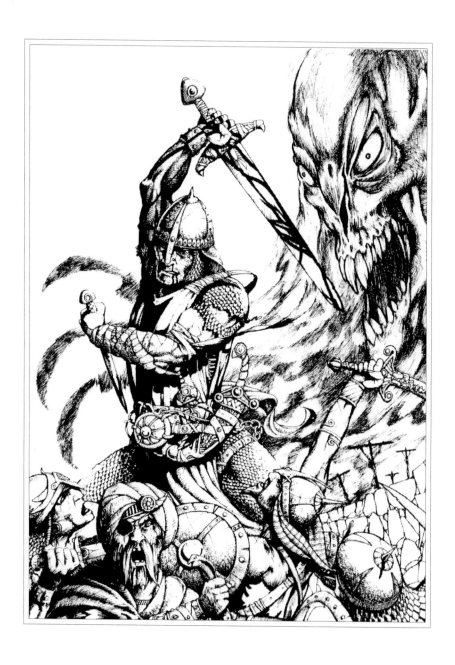

make impact. The way was open for Wulfric, however. The boy came forward with a terrific back-stroke, which if it had caught Navarre on the cranium would have split his head in two. In the last fleeting moment though, Navarre sensed it. He wheeled, parried the blow, then crashed his fist into Wulfric's chin. His attention was drawn from Reynald though, and now the Norman seized the advantage, throwing himself forward and butting Navarre hard on the bridge of the nose.

A scarlet ribbon fell down the Aquitainian's face, and he squawked in outrage, quickly backing away ... and stepping into the gap left by the broken plank, dropping through it to the depth of his thigh. His sword flew from his grasp and his guard was lost, and both Reynald and Wulfric swept in with their own blades, hitting him simultaneously. The knight slashed deeply into Navarre's neck; the boy drove his steel under the flailing left arm, jamming it hard between Navarre's ribs. The baron's man gave a hideous, gargling groan. Black lung-blood sprayed from his mouth, from the wound in his side, from the severed arteries in his neck. He clawed the air, twisting where he was lodged, clearly in intolerable pain.

With an angry curse, but more through mercy than viciousness, Reynald stepped forward again, raised his foot and stamped as hard as he could, twice. An instant later, with a rending crackle of wood, the shattered corpse slipped clean through and dropped into the river.

It vanished quickly, leaving only a purple smudge on the ochre surface.

Was there any person in the world Thurstan could not slay in single combat?

Always before, he'd been able to rely on his prodigious strength, his lightning speed, his precision of hand and eye ... yet now, in the midst of this swirling torrent of heat and dust, the figure which danced before him seemed always to flit out of reach just as his sword struck home. So swiftly did it move that he caught only flickering detail of it ... blink-of-eye glimpses of filed teeth, slanted cat-like eyes, long hands with knife-blade fingernails. This alone, however, was not the deadliest force he dealt with. From all sides, mighty blows were driven into him ... his legs, his arms, his torso. Unseen talons rent and tore. He was thrown in all directions, side to side, up and down, round and round like a dervish ... nauseated, confused, hurled swiftly to the brink of frenzied madness.

He cut and stabbed at the prancing, darting figure with everything he had, but never once did he make contact ... if contact was even possible, and when a savage but invisible fist crashed into his ribs with battering-ram force, and the bones there cracked, the knight knew his death was upon him.

The Leopard of Gerberoi and his brutish son had searched a dozen streets and several empty courts before they noticed the filthied, rotted shades slowly emerging from the dark places between the temples. At first, the men were too incredulous to respond. Moments passed and many more of the diabolic things – the shambling, stinking wrecks – had appeared, by the time awareness finally struck the intruders that the guardians of Uruk at last were stirring.

It might have occurred to Count Sihtric that this, in essence, was stingingly unfair; neither he nor his son had collected so much as pewter goblet yet – they hadn't even found one, if the truth was told – but fairness had never been an important factor in the nobleman's long and violent life. In any case, his thoughts were now otherwise engaged, for as the rancid, crumbling spectres spilled out ant-like from every nook and hidey-hole, cramming the streets in an army of walking putrescence, fully encircling the baron and his wildly-shrieking son, he saw them for what they truly were; formless globs of death itself, each one some lost or forgotten soul, trampled and broken in his own battle-steed's wake, or maybe bled white on the sacrificial slabs of old and barbarous Uruk.

Count Sihtric drew his sword and layed wildly about him … to no avail. The guardians converged steadily, limbless, mindless, surging like the sea; no blade could wound them, no mailed fist stun them. In a silent tide of suffocation, they closed in around the intruders, cloying, all-enveloping, until at last the Leopard's half-choked screech joined that of Joubert's … in abrupt and total silence.

The thing Thurstan fought was virtually invincible. It was lithe and ferocious as a jungle cat, and it now clung to him with irresistible strength as his life ebbed out in ruby rivers. His weapons long broken, the knight could only grapple with it bare-handed, though its slick and oily flesh was firm with iron muscle, invulnerable to his clenching fingers. Every part of the man's body was now bruised, broken, pulped. His vision flashed with stars, a bottomless chasm was opening slowly beneath him.

And then … in an instant, it was over.

But Thurstan wasn't dead. At least … he didn't think he was.

For one incredible second he was a bird, weightless and floating in warm air, the jewelled and rippling Euphrates far below. And then he was a man again, awkward, heavy as clay, plummeting …

He fell faster than he'd ever believed possible, and before he could draw breath, the icy waters hit him with a clap of thunder, enclosing him completely in green and shimmering shadow. For perplexed yet strangely comforting moments, Thurstan drifted there careless, wrapped in fronds and muddy phantasms, and then, the next thing he knew, foul fluid was pouring into his nose and throat, and he was coughing, choking … and suddenly hands were dragging at him, hauling him upwards and out …

Insensible minutes passed, then Thurstan opened his eyes. At once, the pain began … all over his body. He winced, gasped … in the space of a second, he recalled every moment of his fight with the djinn, and he wondered how he'd survived it. 'Surely I'm drowned?' he croaked.

'Almost,' came a tired voice.

Thurstan turned his head left, though it hurt to do so, and saw that he was lying on the shingle shore. Wulfric was sitting there, staring distantly over the river. Some distance behind the boy, Reynald was also visible. The knight's mail was hacked and freshly blood-stained, but he himself seemed unharmed.

'Lucky we saw you,' Wulfric added, in strange, almost disinterested fashion.

With some effort, Thurstan craned his neck forward and saw that he'd been ravaged as if by a wild animal. Scraps of mail and leather remained, but the flesh that was visible was black and blue, and riddled with bleeding gashes. Sensation was returning to his limbs, however, and at length he found he could move. With much cringing, and no little coughing up muck and river-water, he managed to lever himself into a sitting posture. He glanced weakly round: from the row of gibbeted corpses on the far side of the river, he surmised that he was now on the eastern bank. About thirty yards upstream, he saw the rope-bridge. He looked at his rescuers again … they still seemed lost, oddly perplexed.

'Don't tell me,' Thurstan said. 'Not a brick standing on a brick?'

Wulfric shook his head. 'There's nothing there at all … not even rubble. We went through a gully … the same way the baron did. But it's just an empty plain. A wilderness.'

'And where is the baron?'

Again the squire shook his head. 'There's no trace of him. None.'

Thurstan switched his gaze to Reynald. 'And what did you find?'

It took Reynald a moment or two to get his thoughts in order. 'As the boys says, there's nothing there.' He sniffed, then shrugged. 'I doubt there ever was.'

Thurstan was about to reply, when he spotted movement on the higher ground to the east. They followed his gaze and saw Hasif on the crest of the ridge. He was as wind-blown and weather-worn as before, but no longer so cowed. In fact, he was now resting a spear on his shoulder and staring boldly down at them. A minute of such scrutiny passed, then he drew down a strip of turban, wound it about his lower face and strolled out of view.

'He knew what we'd find here,' said Wulfric.

'So did we,' Thurstan replied, climbing painfully to his feet. 'There's no sorcery in that.'

'But why have we been spared?' the boy asked.

Reynald snorted. 'Who says we have?' He pointed west. 'Christendom is a thousand miles that way.'

'We'll get there,' said the boy, moving towards the bridge. 'If God wills it.'

'Aye,' said Thurstan, limping after him. 'Perhaps.' The household champion was feeble from blood-loss, however, and promptly staggered. He would have fallen, had Reynald not put an arm out to him. Their eyes met, Thurstan's registering surprise.

'If God wills it,' Reynald agreed.

THE WINTER HUNT

Steve Lockley & Paul Lewis

Snow tumbled like shreds of paper from a sky the colour of dead flesh. Angharad hated it. Cold weather was never good for her mood but whenever it snowed she always felt worse. Much worse. Neither the central heating nor the glow of the half-smoked Lambert and Butler wedged between her fingers could dispel the chill she felt inside her. The glass of the living room window seemed a flimsy barrier between her and the elements as she stared moodily out at the sliver of grass across the road and, in the distance, the brooding slate-grey sweep of Swansea bay. The green of the roadside verges was already giving way to white with little protest; she knew that if the snow started to settle on the roads, too, then the buses would soon give up the fight and she would have to walk into work.

Not that it was such a great job, sales assistant in a discount shoe shop. Still, if the pay was little more than minimum wage, at least the girls there were a good laugh. And, besides, anything was better than spending a day in the house with Dad and his filthy, hungover temper. She would have asked Gareth for a lift except the sod hadn't come home last night. Out on the piss with Mark, no doubt. Angharad cursed them. One of the selfish bastards could have had the decency to ring and let her know where they were, tell her not to worry. For all she knew they could have spent the night in the cells at Swansea Central, her brother and her boyfriend banged up together. Serves them right if they had. Maybe something like that would be just the shock they needed to stop them from pulling another stupid stunt. If they had been caught, well tough. It would be no fault of hers.

'Shit!' she said to herself, stubbing out the cigarette in a chipped glass ashtray that bore the legend A Present from Barry Island and a picture of a funfair. For a moment she was swept away to a better place and time, when they had been together as a family. Mum before she decided she'd had enough of dad's drinking and ran off with a shop fitter from Cardiff; Dad before the booze had become so attractive; Gareth still wearing shorts and finding fun in everything; and herself before she had any cares in the world. Christ, she hated her life but she was trapped, having deliberately cut off any means of escape years ago. She had not so much made her bed as dug her own shallow grave. Angharad had loved school and all the teachers assured her getting sufficient grades for a college place was merely a formality. Despite this she had left as soon as the law allowed, working her fingers to the bone holding down job after crappy job to support Gareth after Mum left. And how had he repaid her? By letting her down, walking over her time after time. These days he never even said thanks whenever Angharad did anything for him, which was often, despite his constant thoughtlessness.

The sound of Dad puking upstairs brought her back to reality. Angharad turned on the TV for a moment, to drown the noise. Usually she preferred a silent house in the morning; no TV, no radio, a rare chance for a few moments of peace. Right now, though, she needed company, even if it was just the face and voice of a stranger on the flat screen. The local news was just ending, but she caught a snatch as the camera zoomed in on a burnt-out car in a field of snow. Another one she thought. Is that all they have to show? It seemed that cars were being stolen every day and ending up torched on waste ground somewhere. This one had been dumped in Penllergaer Woods, taking out a chunk of forest with it. Angharad switched the set off and went back to the window.

The sky was getting heavier by the minute and she knew it was now or never. It would be easy enough to walk back home later even if the snow lay a foot deep, but the steep gradient of Mount Pleasant Hill would become too treacherous to even attempt to get down if she left it much longer. Slipping her cigarettes and green plastic lighter into her handbag, Angharad took her coat from the newel post at the bottom of the stairs where it had been buried beneath her dad's stained and stinking anorak. She brushed it down violently. As she pushed one arm into a sleeve the telephone rang.

'Annie?' said a panicky voice down the line.

'Gareth?' Of course it was him, it was bound to be. Nobody else would ring at that time of the morning. It was still only eight. 'Where the hell are you?'

'The station.'

So she'd been right. 'And what did they get you for this time?'

'Not the nick,' he replied without a trace of reproach. 'The train station.'

'You've been there all night?'

'Just about,' he said.

'But why?' She already suspected he had been on the piss in Cardiff and had missed the last train home. 'Is Mark with you?'

'He was. He's gone now.'

'What're you talking about? Why has he gone?'

'Maybe he's braver than I am.'

Angharad felt her grip on the receiver tighten through a combination of frustration and fear. Something was wrong, that much was obvious. If only Gareth would cut the crap and just tell her what. She forced herself to be calm. 'Braver? Come on, Gareth, spit it out. What sort of trouble have you two been getting into?' For a moment she was ashamed at the way she'd just assumed they'd been up to no good. But then, why shouldn't she? She had lost count of the number of times the police had called round because Gareth had been fighting or caught shoplifting. She was on first-name terms with a couple of them.

'You wouldn't believe me if I told you.'

'I haven't got time for this,' she snapped. 'Some of us have to go to work.'

'Yeah, all right. Sorry.' There was a momentary pause. When Gareth spoke the words came out slowly, as if for once in his life he was thinking about what he said before he said it. 'I just need to know if you'd seen anything funny going on. You know, like anyone hanging around the house or anything.'

'Shit, Gareth –'

The first thing she thought of was that he'd gotten mixed up with drugs, that he owed someone money and now they were after him for it. Unfair, she knew, because while he was hardly whiter than white, Gareth had never been into drugs, not even grass. Booze and fags, yeah, big-time, but not drugs. Yet she knew he was easily influenced. Gareth could be talked into anything. If Mark had put him up to it, she'd kill him.

'It's all right,' he said quickly. 'I didn't mean anything heavy.'

'What, then?' Angharad demanded. As far as she was concerned her brother could get into as much trouble as he wanted. But she didn't want him dragging it home.

'Probably nothing. I thought I saw ... I thought I saw some lads hanging around, that's all. Remember when that gang beat Simon Harrington up to get his money? I was worried this lot might be trying to do the same thing to me.'

Oh yeah, Angharad thought. Like you worry about anything. Pity you didn't start worrying now and then. Maybe then you wouldn't be in the shit all the time. She could not even be bothered to respond to the lie. 'I haven't seen anything like that,' she sighed.

The relief in his voice was evident, even down the line. 'Thank Christ for that. I owe you one, Annie.' His nickname for her. ' I'll be home as soon as I can, all right?'

'Whatever. I'll be gone before you get here. And you hear from that little shit Mark ... tell him to forget tonight.' It wasn't so much the fact that he hadn't been in touch; she'd gotten used to that. Her schoolgirl dreams of a handsome man who would sweep her off her feet and love her forever had been reduced to faint memory. Sure, Mark was nice enough in a rough diamond kind of way, better in fact than most of the men she'd known. Great body, didn't knock her about, bought her nice presents. Problem was, he took her for granted, expected her to come running whenever he clicked his fingers. Well, sod that. And sod Mark, too. She was already so fed up of his coming and going that she was planning to dump him before long. It would be easier that way. 'If he thinks he can waltz in and out whenever it suits him, you tell him he can just forget it, okay?'

'Sure,' Gareth said, sounding as if he'd heard this too many times before. Which he probably had, Angharad thought with a flicker of self-disgust. She was full of talk, oh sure, but when it came to the crunch, she was the one who backed down. Every time.

Her thoughts masked the cold as she walked with exaggerated care along Pantycelin and into Mount Pleasant. The council gritters rarely ventured this far from the main roads through the city, especially the hospital routes. Patches of ice lay hidden beneath the snow to catch the unwary. Once a bus passed her with a sound resembling rushing water as its wheels scythed through the slush on the road. For a moment Angharad thought about flagging it down but then decided against it. She would get to work far too early and, besides, despite her hatred of the cold, she found to her surprise that she was actually enjoying the walk. Her legs ached and her chest was not too clever – bloody cigarettes; she'd have to give them up – but she could live with that. The thing was, the more she walked, the less troubled her thoughts became, as if each step she took away from home put further distance between Angharad and her problems as well.

By the time she returned it was mid-afternoon and darkness was already exerting its grip on the world. Snow had fallen relentlessly all day. As the hours had passed, so the flow of customers had dried up. When Angharad had ventured outside to check on the weather, Oxford Street was like a white desert. Finally, the manager had decided to send them all home and shut up early. Now, struggling back up Mount Pleasant, Angharad wished to God another bus would pass her by. Thick flakes of snow blinded her, driven into her eyes by a vicious wind that hoisted the ends of the scarf she had knotted around her neck and caused them to dance in the air like charmed snakes.

A building, big and dark, loomed out of the oscillating whiteness as she trudged up the never-ending hill; St Jude's. Snow had covered the church's ledges, filled its crevices and blanketed its roof. It resembled the fairy tale-like Bavarian castle that had graced her favourite childhood jigsaw. She paused outside it for a moment, catching her breath. Despite the burning in her chest she was gasping for a cigarette but there was no chance. A cup of coffee, a fag, and the gas fire turned up high; the sole reasons for her wanting to be back home. There sure as hell was nothing else to look forward to. If this kept up the old man would even have to miss his trip to the pub and would that put him in a bad mood. Angharad sighed and moved on.

Soon her leg muscles were aching like never before. At one point she lost her footing and went sprawling, the snow which had hampered her every step of the way now offering no resistance as she fell through it. Angharad landed heavily on her left wrist, biting down a yell of pain. She held her left hand tenderly with her right, moving it about. It did not feel broken but it hurt like hell all the same. Self-pity swamped her. Christ, she wished she could find some way out of this miserable existence of hers. It was more like a life sentence than a life. Gareth, Mark, her old man ... they had their means of escape, either through recklessness or drunkenness. Yeah, she thought bitterly, they had found their freedom but her ties to them meant she could never have hers. As she sat miserably in the snow the sound of the wind changed pitch, deepening as if in response to her mood, becoming dark and mournful. Angharad felt close to tears and it took every ounce of determination she possessed for her to get up and press on. The cold intensified, slicing through her thick winter clothes and boots until her body was forced to shiver almost constantly in an effort to keep itself warm. Where had this blizzard come from? Certainly it hadn't been on the weather forecast. It was the worst snowfall Angharad could remember. Maybe all those warnings about global warming were true. Maybe the climate really was screwed up. What if this was nature's way at getting back at them for the damage they had inflicted? Whatever, it seemed wrong.

Anxiety swelled inside her. Several times she thought she saw low, dark shapes scurrying past on the other side of the white veil. These she dismissed as illusions, which she attributed to her state of mind and the arctic wind that caused her vision to blur. By the time she reached home she was so exhausted her anxiety had turned to panic. Her fingers trembled so badly that she barely managed to retrieve the door key from her bag and slip it into the lock. The key turned smoothly but when the pushed at the door it would not move. She stared at it for a moment, until her cold-numbed brain finally realised some-one must have slipped the security clip on, locking her out.

Crying with frustration, she hammered on the double-glazed panel with her right hand, hugging her aching left to her chest. 'Gareth!' she called. 'Come on – open up!'

No reply. Angharad called again without response and gingerly made her way through the deep snow in front of the house until she reached the window. She pressed her face against the glass and peered inside. The curtains were drawn almost closed; she was certain they had been open when she'd left. Of course they had been, she reminded herself. She distinctly remembered looking out as the blizzard started. Squinting through the narrow chink she could just make out the prostrate shape of her brother stretched out on the settee. She rapped her key on the glass and with a sense of savage satisfaction saw Gareth sit bolt upright with a start, knocking over a can of lager he'd placed on the floor as he did so. He looked around, then straight at the window.

'Open the door, you drunken git!' she yelled, furious with him.

'Annie?' His voice was muffled through the double-glazed pane.

'Expecting someone else?' Then she recalled the conversation they'd had earlier. Of course he'd been expecting someone else. Someone he was afraid of, who was going to come around and kick seven shades out of him. She heard a sharp click as the safety clip was disconnected, then the front door swung open. Gareth stared out at her. His skin was pallid, his eyes wide and tinged with red. He could have been half-drunk or half-asleep. Then again, she thought with a twinge of sympathy that quickly mutated to anger, maybe he was afraid.

Whatever trouble he was in, she didn't want to know. One thing she knew from bitter experience; there was no point trying to help her brother. He didn't want to be helped. Whenever she said anything, he'd accuse her of interfering. If he wanted to live life his own way, fine. As long as he didn't come crying to her when things went wrong, as they no doubt had now. Best to let him learn his own lessons.

He went to speak as she staggered through the doorway but she pushed right past him, heading for the stairs. The snow on her clothes melted as she ascended, droplets of water cascading from her and soaking the carpet below. She didn't care. Her face and hands burned as circulation returned. The pain was so intense she almost cried out aloud when she reached the bathroom and attempted to undress. Finally she managed it and set the shower for as hot as she could tolerate. It felt wonderful, a blast of molten metal that stripped the cold from her skin. Steam boiled around her, filling the small room until she could barely see a hand in front of her face.

Dressed, and with a towel wrapped round her hair, Angharad went downstairs. The living room was in darkness. She switched on the light and saw that Gareth was still on the settee, sat up this time, watching her warily as she crossed to the window. She pulled back the curtains. It was almost night. Beyond her own ghostly mirror image she saw a flickering of white as the snow steadily fell. For some reason it transfixed her.

'There's tea on the table for you,' Gareth said quietly, breaking the spell.

Angharad turned and picked up the mug. She sipped at the tea and, while it had obviously been sitting there for several minutes, it still felt deliciously warm. It was, she knew, intended to be a peace offering. Okay. She'd buy it. For now.

'Where's the old man?' she asked.

'Two guesses.'

'Jesus. On a night like this?'

'Take more than a blizzard to keep him from his booze.'

'True,' Angharad said. The resignation she felt was depressing. So this was what her life had boiled down to. A council semi on a lousy estate with a troublemaker for a brother and a drunkard for a father. What she wouldn't give to find a way out. She sat in disheartened silence for a moment, then looked at her brother. Her resolution to make him sort his own mess crumbled at sight of the forlorn expression on his face. She sighed. Gareth wouldn't be twenty for another few months, nearly ten years her junior. She'd acted more mum than big sister since their own mother had left. It was hard to stop now.

'You going tell me what this is all about?' she said.

Gareth glanced away, refusing to meet her gaze. 'There's nothing going on.'

'Of course something's going on. You spend the night freezing your arse off in the train station then lock yourself in the house. Are you going to tell me?'

'It was safe.'

'What was safe?'

'The station. There are lights on all night.'

'You could have had the lights on here, where it's warm.'

'We couldn't get here. There wouldn't have been time.'

'Come on, Gareth. Who was it?'

He looked up at her and Angharad could see genuine fear in his eyes. 'I don't know,' he said. 'But they got Monkey.'

'Monkey Jackson? You didn't say he was with you.'

He shrugged.

Angharad felt the anger rising inside her. She wanted to take her brother's shoulders and shake some sense into him. Having him hang around with Mark was just about tolerable. But not Monkey. He was an evil bastard, that one. As soon as his name was mentioned Angharad knew that whatever shit Gareth was mixed up in, it was serious. Monkey didn't dabble in petty crime. Anything he was involved with was heavy. He not only attracted trouble like a magnet, he seemed to revel in it. 'What in Christ's name is wrong with you?' she said. 'I've told you to keep clear of Monkey. He's bad news.'

'Yeah well,' Gareth said. 'I won't be going near him again, not after tonight.'

He closed his eyes. Angharad, sensing he was on the verge of telling her what the hell was going on, sat back in the chair and waited silently. Finally Gareth spoke. 'Monkey nicked a Fiesta from over in Killay,' he said. 'An XR2.'

'I should have known,' Angharad said, mouth a thin, angry line.

'You going to let me finish this?'

'I don't know if I want to.'

'Fine. I didn't want to talk about it. You're the one who kept on.'

'All right,' Angharad said testily, still annoyed with him.

So he told her.

They'd been round Mark's house, chilling out, listening to the new Chemical Brothers CD when the phone rang. It was Monkey, calling from his mobile. Said he'd lifted a Fiesta and dumped it on Mynyddbach Common. Trouble was, he needed a lift back to Townhilll. Mark told him to get stuffed, it was too fucking cold. Gareth had no idea what Monkey said after that but it was enough to make Mark change his mind. When he asked if Gareth wanted to come for the ride, Gareth said sure. Nothing better to do.

So they cruised along in Mark's Cavalier, taking their time, hoping Monkey would have given up and called a taxi before they arrived. No such luck. Monkey was not only there, he was pissed. He was so cold he'd run across to the King's Head and knocked back a few pints and a few vodkas for good measure. The Fiesta's bonnet was still ticking metallically as the engine cooled down. Monkey had probably floored the pedal all the way here. Stupid bastard was at the back of the car, giggling like a loon. Gareth wondered what he found so funny. Then Monkey's lighter sparked into life, the flame supernaturally bright, and Gareth saw the Fiesta's petrol cap had been broken off and a rag stuffed inside. Monkey had winked at him, then, and told him to run. The last thing Gareth saw before he spun around and legged it was the rag bursting into flames.

He was vaguely aware of Mark running to his right he raced across the common, away from the road and the possibility of being seen. Monkey was way behind them, laughing crazily. Gareth looked back, expecting to see the car explode. It didn't, though thick black smoke was belching into the dark sky. He stumbled to a halt, heart racing frantically, chest killing him. Mark drew up alongside him, gasped something about Monkey being a fucking psychopath, which was when they heard them. The dogs. It sounded like dozens of the things, a wild barking which drew steadily closer. The writhing column of smoke from the car began to swirl as if it were being spun around by the wind, this despite the fact that the night air was utterly still. Then it seemed to collapse to the ground, rolling across the common until it surrounded them like a sea.

A man came striding out of the darkness. The sound of the dogs was deafening now. Gareth's mind went blank. His brain felt pierced by the incessant noise. He squinted at the man but could not make out his features. He was tall and built like a brick shithouse, that much Gareth could see. The man turned as Monkey came blundering through the smoke towards him, coughing harshly and calling for them. He was no longer laughing. What happened next seemed to Gareth to happen in slow motion.

The man raised an arm and the smoke was torn asunder, streamers of it ripping off and spiralling away as countless dark shapes raced from all directions towards Monkey. He looked over towards Gareth, eyes wide with terror, and then, with a startled yell that echoed around the common, he was suddenly pulled to the ground. The barking ceased, to be replaced by a cacophony of snarls and growls that could not quite mask Monkey's screams. The hideous cries chilled Gareth to the bone. He could not move, could not speak. All he could do was wait in dumb terror for the hounds to turn on him.

He heard Mark yell at him, but the words sounded distant and muffled. Then a fist crashed against the side of his head, breaking the spell. Gareth blinked, saw Mark running, set off in pursuit without even stopping to think about it. All he wanted to do was get away from that terrible place while he was still in one piece. He couldn't see the ground beneath his feet and later he would feel cold and sick when he thought about how easily he could have fallen, breaking something maybe, left to lie there helplessly like bait in a trap until the dogs had finished with Monkey and turned their attention to him.

But he made it.

Christ alone knew how, but he made it.

He'd barely shut the door behind him when Mark rammed the gear stick into first. The Cavalier shot forward with a screech of tyres, the sudden acceleration slamming Gareth back against the passenger seat. They raced from the common, risking being seen by the cops, until they were at least a couple of miles away. Only then did Mark ease the pressure on the pedal and they were travelling at more or less the legal limit. Neither of them said anything. Gareth knew he sure as hell didn't know what had gone on back there and he doubted Mark was any the wiser. It had all happened so quickly it did not seem real. Then he remembered the sound of Monkey's screaming as the pack had torn into him and it suddenly seemed far more real than he wanted it to. Then Mark said fuck in a strangely quiet voice, his eyes fixed on the rear-view mirror.

Gareth jerked round in his seat until he could see out of the back window.

Dense mist swirled from one side of the road to the other. Through it Gareth saw a jumble of dark shapes, low to the ground. Myriad pinpoints of red light pierced the miasma and he instinctively knew they were eyes.   Behind them, rising above the writhing mist like some ancient colossus, was the man from the common. There was no mistaking him. Impossible as it was, dogs and man alike were keeping pace with the car – no, they were gaining on it. Mark swore again. The engine roared, a growl so deep Gareth felt as if the fillings in his mouth would tear themselves out of his teeth. He clutched the sides of his seat as the Cavalier picked up speed, racing along the deserted streets until it was flying like a bat out of hell through the night. Gareth twisted round again. The pack was still in pursuit but with a huge sense of relief he saw it had fallen behind. Before he knew it they were screaming down High Street and then Mark pumped the brakes as they drew up to the railway station. He steered the Cavalier recklessly into one of the taxi bays outside the shabby entrance, hauled on the handbrake, then threw open his door the moment the car came to a halt. Gareth followed swiftly behind.

They took refuge in the station, hastily concocting a cover story in case they were challenged. Everything was shut up for the night so they were forced to perch uncomfortably on the frozen edge of one of the platform benches, shivering, smoking constantly in a futile effort to keep the cold at bay. They sat so that they kept the main entrance in view, ready to bolt at the first sign of the dogs. More than once Gareth was sure he saw dark shapes scuttle through the pre-dawn light outside but they disappeared like ghosts each time he rubbed his eyes. He was on the verge of dozing off despite the chills that wracked his body, when Mark lunged to his feet and fished the Cavalier keys from his pocket. Stay here, he ordered. I'll be back soon.

He turned his back on Gareth's protests and strode out of the station.

Gareth had never in his life felt as alone or as terrified as he did right then.

There was no doubt in Angharad's mind that her brother was telling the truth. Or, at least, the truth as he saw it. His voice was hoarse as he recounted his story; on more than one occasion it cracked and she knew he was close to tears. He'd been genuinely afraid, of that she was certain. The question was, afraid what of? Gareth was scared of dogs, had been since he'd been a kid. A neighbour's Labrador, normally a loll-tongued, good-natured thing, had snapped at Gareth when the five-year-old boy had run up to it too quickly while playing. It was more scratch than bite but it had left mental scars that lasted long after the physical had faded. Maybe there had been a man on Mynyddbach Common, out walking his own dogs. Had Monkey known about Gareth's phobia – which was likely; he seemed to know everything about everyone – it was equally feasible he had been taking the piss, putting on an act to scare the younger boys. The bastard probably got off on stupid games like that. As for the rest, well, adrenalin coupled with booze could have conjured up all kinds of phantoms. As long as it was just booze. Not drugs. She couldn't cope with that. Neither could she ask him outright, not right then. He was too upset. Before she could say anything there was a loud rapping on the front door. Gareth started and again Angharad could see the raw terror in his eyes.

'It's all right,' she said. 'Madmen with packs of dogs are not likely to knock.' She said it with a smile but her jocular approach had no visible calming effect.

It was obvious Gareth had no intention of getting the door so, with a groan that echoed the silent protest of her muscles, she pushed herself up from the chair and limped into the hallway. Through the glass panes she could see a tall, dark figure, standing close to the door. A fragment of Gareth's story flickered into her mind and, as ridiculous as it was, she felt a tingle of unease as she reached for the lock. 'Who is it?' she called.

'Me,' Mark answered. 'Let us in. It's bastard freezing out here.'

As soon as she heard his voice Angharad felt the resentment that had gnawed at her since she'd arrived home suddenly flare into outright anger. She pulled the door open and, as Mark staggered into the house, an avalanche of snow cascading from his black leather jacket, she put her hand to his chest and pushed him up against the hallway wall with a force that surprised her and provoked a grunt of astonished surprise from him.

'Christ – '

'You bastard,' she hissed, not wanting Gareth to hear.

Mark shook his head while he pawed ineffectually at Angharad's hand. 'Give us a chance to get through the sodding door. What in hell's name has gotten into you?'

'You left him,' Angharad said. 'Anything could have happened.'

'But that's why I left him. To make sure he was safe.'

He sounded genuine enough to confuse her. 'Safe? Who from?'

'The dogs,' Mark said helplessly. 'Hasn't he told you yet?'

Angharad felt the anger melt away as quickly as the snow that was now little more than a Rorschach test on the carpet. She relaxed her grip. 'He told me.'

Tugging his jacket down around him, Mark edged past her and into the living room. 'Here,' he said, holding out a rolled-up newspaper which

Angharad snatched off him without looking at it. Her mind was too busy concentrating on what she would say to him and her brother the moment she had them together. She turned away to close the door, glancing out into the street as she did. Snow appeared as cones of static beneath the fog-smeared streetlights. The world seemed utterly still, utterly quiet. A dog's deep bark suddenly tore through the silence and Angharad, shivering, hastily pushed the door shut.

Gareth and Mark sat at opposite ends of the sofa, eyes downcast, like lovers after an argument. The pair of them looked so dejected Angharad's determination to discover what they had really been up to momentarily weakened. But then she recalled her own fury at the way they had treated her, vanishing overnight without so much as a word.

No, she told herself. They're not going to get off the hook this time.

'So,' she said, standing before them. 'What happened?'

Gareth glared up at her. 'I already told you.'

''For God's sake, you think I'm going to fall for that crap?'

'But it's true!'

'Last chance,' she said. 'Tell me. Or tell the old man when he gets back.'

Gareth's eyes held hers, as if he thought he could win the argument by staring her down. In the periphery of her vision Angharad saw Mark shrug out of his leather jacket and drop it to the side of the settee. 'Read the paper,' she heard him say.

'What?'

'The paper,' Mark said. 'The one I gave you. Read it.'

She gave him a poisonous look, then unfolded that night's *Evening Post*. At first the words on the front page failed to register before her brain made sense of what her eyes were seeing and the headline jumped out at her like one of those Magic Eye 3-D puzzles. It said, in large bold print:

CITY MAN FOUND MURDERED

The paper nearly fell from her suddenly trembling hands.

She read the story, then read it again and a third time before it finally sunk in. Barry Jackson, nicknamed Monkey, was dead. His body had been found just after dawn next to a burnt-out car on Mynyddbach Common. The body was so badly charred as to be unrecognisable, but police had ruled out an accident. Despite the severity of the burns Monkey's body was covered in deep wounds, possibly inflicted by a knife or other sharp object. The case was being treated as murder. Witnesses were urged to come forward.

I never knew his real name was Barry, Angharad thought, and had to bite back a laugh she knew she would find almost impossible to stop.

'You all right?' she heard Gareth ask, as if from a great distance.

'Yeah,' she said, shaking her head to clear it. She lowered herself into the chair and folded the paper carefully before placing it on her lap. 'I think so.'

'Now do you believe us?' Mark said. 'I mean, Monkey's dead, right? If that part of what Gareth told you is true, why shouldn't the rest of it be?'

'Because it all sounds so crazy,' Angharad shouted back, her previous urge to laugh now a near-compulsion to cry. 'That's why.'

Gareth reached over and gripped her shoulder. 'I know, Annie. It's crazy, but it really did happen that way. Why do you think we would make up a story like that?'

'Yeah,' said Mark. 'We had nothing to do with what happened to Monkey, all right? But if we did, you can guarantee we'd come up with a decent fucking lie.'

'Okay, okay,' Angharad said, pressing her hands to her ears. 'I believe you.'

And she did. Even if it made her a prime candidate for one of the mental wards at Cefn Coed Hospital, she believed them. Gareth had been many things over the years but he had never lied to her. Neither, to the best of her knowledge, had Mark. And their point about coming up with a better story if they'd wanted to rang absolutely true. Why come up with such a cock and bull tale when they could easily have said nothing? If they'd told her they'd been partying in Cardiff all night, she would have accepted it without question.

No, God help her, she believed them.

And with that certainty she felt her old strength return. She would get Gareth out of this. One way or another she'd pull him out of the shit like she had so many times when they'd been growing up. Mark, too, if he'd let her. But first there was something she needed to know. 'Why did you leave him?' she asked.

Mark frowned. 'Monkey? We didn't have much choice'

'No, not Monkey. Gareth. Why did you leave him at the station?'

'I was trying to protect him.' Mark shifted uncomfortably on the settee. 'It was my fault he was there. I felt pretty shitty about that so I got back in the car and drove off. They hadn't made any attempt to get into the station, so I reckoned Gareth'd be safe. I thought they'd come after me but there was no sign of them anywhere.'

'I didn't know,' Gareth said. 'I just thought you'd done a runner.'

Mark looked hurt. 'No way, man. I drove round and round for bloody ages. Then I thought, right, coast's clear. They've given up I got back to the station and you'd gone. I tried phoning you all day but there was no answer. Then the snow started and ...'

'You came up to check,' Angharad said.

'Yeah, well, anyway, I thought maybe there was something wrong with the lines. I tell you, I'm really fucking glad the two of you are okay.'

'Thanks,' Angharad said.

'Don't mention it.'

She got up from her chair and bent over Mark, planting a kiss on his cheek. 'I mean it. Thanks.' She sat on the arm of the settee next to him and ran her fingers through his hair, remembering why it was she had been attracted to him in the first place. Sure, he could be a bastard but equally he was capable of unexpected, disarming acts of kindness.

'So what are we going to do now?' Gareth asked.

'Stay put,' Mark said. 'Keep our mouths shut. All of this will blow over.'

'That's not the answer,' Angharad told them. 'Go to the cops.'

'The police?' Mark looked appalled. 'You mad, or what?'

'Think about it,' Angharad insisted. 'You go to them, tell them what you saw. Yeah, they'll question you but they'll let you go in the end. There's nothing to tie you to Monkey's death, and you came forward of your own free will. That counts for a lot.'

'You obviously don't know the fucking local law,' Gareth sneered.

'No, but I know what'll happen if someone saw you running from the common or driving off and the police manage to track you down. Before long they'll find out you and Monkey were old mates. They'll want to know why you didn't come forward if you had nothing to hide. Next thing, the two of you'll be done for murder. That what you want?'

'They won't be able to prove nothing,' Mark said defiantly.

'Oh, get real.' Angharad's voice was shrill with exasperation. 'If they want evidence, they'll make sure they find it. Read the papers, Mark. It happens all the time.'

'They'll do us for nicking the car.' Gareth said.

Angharad did not miss the venomous look Mark cast her brother's way. 'Why would they do you for nicking the car? You weren't involved.'

Then she could almost feel cogs begin to turn in her head as connections began to be made. Heat radiated from her cheeks. 'You stupid bastards,' she said, restraining her fury. 'It's been you all along, hasn't it?'

'Dunno what you're on about,' Gareth said, without looking at her.

'All those stolen cars being dumped and set on fire. No wonder you don't want to go to the police. They'll do you if they know you've been involved.'

'They won't find out,' Mark said. He had the sense not to bother

86

denying it, yet equally Angharad wanted to reach out and slap the smug, almost arrogant expression off his face. 'Not if we keep our traps shut. I told you, all this will blow over before long.'

'And what if the dogs come back? What if they're out there now, waiting?'

She might just as well have slapped him. His self-assurance visibly crumbled as her words hit home. The sight of Mark displaying such naked fear was the final proof, if any more were needed, they had been telling the truth all along. 'Exactly,' she said. 'If you go to the police you'll be protected. Well, a lot safer than you are now, anyway.'

'Like they're going to believe us,' Gareth said morosely. 'A pack of dogs coming out of nowhere, that big bastard leading them. All we'll get from the cops is a drugs test.'

He had a point, though Angharad would never say as much aloud. She sensed they were ready to go along with her just as soon as their stupid macho egos would allow them. All she had to do was keep coaxing and play down any of their concerns.

'Don't tell them everything you saw. Just parts of it.'

That sounded good. It certainly caught their interest, so she continued hurriedly, making it up as she went along. 'Tell them about Monkey's phone call. Say he wanted a lift from the King's Head back home. He told you he'd be waiting for you on the road by the common, but when you turn up there's no sign of him.' She paused, gathering her thoughts.

'Then what?' Mark asked.

'Shut up, I'm thinking. Okay, so you drive off. You don't see any car on fire, but you notice a man walking his dogs on the common. Nasty-looking dogs. Pit bulls, say. It stuck in your mind because it seemed too late and too cold for anyone to be out walking.'

The torrent of words dried up. Angharad shrugged and fell silent.
Mark raised a disbelieving eyebrow. 'That's it?'

'The simpler you keep it, the better,' she insisted. 'Easier to get your stories straight that way. Besides, like you said, the moment you start telling them about a mist coming out of nowhere and killer dogs chasing you all the way into Swansea they'll bang you up until they reckon the shit has had a chance to work its way out of your system.'

She waited for more objections. None was forthcoming, thank God.

'All right,' she said slowly, suddenly aware that her shoulder muscles were so tense they almost hurt and forcing them to relax. She was in control of the situation now. All she had to do was lead by example and keep calm. Maybe then Mark and Gareth would do the same and they could get all this sorted out with a minimum of fuss. She turned to Mark. 'Did you manage to get the car up the hill?'

'Yeah. It's parked on the drive.'

'Good. Get your coats on. We're going.'

Gareth looked at her as if she were crazy. 'In this weather. Come off it.'

'Fine,' Angharad said. 'But if you want me to go with you, it's now or never.'

Gareth and Mark swapped glances. Neither of them even bothered to protest. They both knew as well as she did that they could never talk their way out of this without her around to support them. Mark reached down and snatched up his coat from the floor with ill-disguised annoyance. He pulled the keys from the pocket and Angharad held out her hand. 'I'll drive,' she said. 'You morons are in enough trouble as it is.'

The snow seemed to have eased off a little when they got outside. Gareth slid into the back of the Cavalier and Mark thumped down into the front seat with such force as to leave Angharad in no doubt he was seriously pissed off with her. Well, bollocks to him. He drove like an idiot at the best of times and Angharad was not about to risk her neck trying to get his off the chopping block. She didn't own a car, couldn't afford one on her pay, but Gareth let her use his Escort when he didn't need it and Angharad reckoned she was a pretty safe driver. To her relief the engine started first time and she reversed out of the drive and into the road. The wet rumble of slush beneath the wheels made her afraid keeping control would be a problem. She needn't have worried. The slow and steady passage of cars had melted much of the snow and a number of people had shovelled sand from the yellow roadside box to improve conditions outside their own homes. As long as the temperature didn't fall, freezing them over, the roads should be passable with care.

'You sure you don't want me to drive?' Mark said, wiping the windscreen in front of him with the back of his hand. His tone was conciliatory. 'Weather's shit.'

'I'm okay,' said Angharad. 'It's not as bad as I thought.'

'Yeah it's weird all right,' she heard Gareth say from the back. 'The snow's still coming down real heavy but it doesn't look like it's sticking any more.'

Angharad squinted through the frosted glass. It was odd. She'd expected the main roads through the town to be kept clear but was surprised the gritters had ventured this far down the side streets. But she could clearly see the black of the tarmac that stretched out before her and the pale contrast of the pavements running parallel. There was nothing, no ice or snow to obscure them. Something else caught her eye. The roofs of the houses were free of snow, yet the lawns below them were covered in white and the trees which lined the road resembled skeletal hands dressed in ermine gloves.

She could not explain it, but it disturbed her deeply.

'Why are we going this way?' Mark asked when they reached the end of the road and he realised Angharad was not taking them the direct route into town.

'I'm not risking Mount Pleasant Hill,' she said. 'You might get a thrill out of taking stupid risks but I don't. One patch of black ice and we're all screwed.'

Closing her mind to his exasperated sigh, Angharad concentrated on the road. The snow may have cleared, for whatever reason, but as she drove through the estate so she must have hit a pocket of mist, for the landscape around them suddenly lost definition as if they had entered some other, ghostly realm. She slowed her speed, swearing softly to herself, and gripped the wheel tightly. She hated driving in fog as much as she hated driving along narrow country lanes; hated that sense of not being fully in control, of not knowing what unexpected obstacles could be lying in wait just around the corner. The mist reversed her perspective, making the car seem stationary and the world appear to be in motion. Broken lines of parked cars drifted by like misshapen barges. The long terraces of council houses, which she knew to be only a few yards either side of her, suddenly seemed to shrink into the distance, their lights diminishing in size and intensity as the fog noticeably thickened. I don't like this, she thought. I don't like this one bit.

'Oh Christ,' she heard Gareth stage-whisper, and at first she thought he shared her dismay at this latest downturn in the weather. Her eyes darted to the rear-view mirror, which was angled for a driver of Mark's height, not hers, so that she could see how her brother had twisted and was staring out of the back window. Angharad reached up and swivelled the mirror until she had an unobstructed view of the road behind. It revealed what appeared to be a thick grey bank, as if the fog had been squeezed into a dense rectangular block, its frayed and uneven edges constantly unravelling and spiralling away into the night as the dark mass rushed silently down the street after them. Deep within the haze Angharad saw a starscape of red lights blazing with the piercing intensity of lasers. Towering over it was the unmistakable, yet impossibly large, figure of a man. She had told Gareth and Mark she believed their story, and she had, she really had. But believing someone out of love or blind faith was one thing. Seeing it, actually seeing it right before her very own eyes, was something else entirely. It was like the difference between seeing someone knocked down in real life and seeing it happen on TV. No matter how realistic the dramatised version, it could not hold a candle to the sickening immediacy of reality.

She gasped, and Mark twisted towards her. 'What now?'

Then he too looked behind. 'Fuck,' he cried. 'Get us out of here!'

If there was any doubt in Angharad's mind about what to do, the undisguised fear in his voice was enough to spur her into action. She floored the accelerator, breathing a sigh of relief as she felt the tyres grip the slushy road surface. The Cavalier leapt forward with a metallic growl. Instinct, the overwhelming urge to flee in the face of imminent danger, had taken over, controlling Angharad with the same unthinking efficiency that she now worked the controls of the car. She grappled with her terror, aware she was driving way too fast. The shock of what she had seen behind them left her disorientated, so that she was not certain of their exact whereabouts. How far along the road had they travelled? Had they climbed the hill and gone past the sharp turn that could send them hurtling over the edge and down the steep drop if she misjudged? Angharad realised she was more afraid of what was in pursuit than she was of killing of all three of them. But that was stupid. One thing rapidly became clear; if they crashed they would be totally exposed and vulnerable. Easy targets for whatever was giving chase.

A sudden flash like a bolt of lightning filled the night sky around them. Speed camera, Angharad thought, checking the speedo out of habit. She was not surprised it hovered around sixty. Neither did she particularly care. By now she was sufficiently calm to realise exactly where on the estate they were so she kept her foot down hard until they reached the twin mini-roundabouts at the bottom of the hill. Without hesitating she swung the car left through the first then right through the second. Only when she reach the third roundabout did she put pressure on the brakes, realising with a rising sensation of horror that her mind was as frozen as the landscape outside. She had no idea which direction she should be heading. Not even the sight of blurred motion in the rear-view mirror could shake the sense of lassitude that gripped her. 'Where the hell do I go now?'

Mark gave her a frightened glance. It could have been due to her bleakly helpless tone or the prospect of them being overtaken 'Straight on and keep going through the lights. Get onto Oystermouth road. It's faster. We should be able to outrun them.'

'Right.' It sounded good, a damn sight better than her own plan which was to pinch herself in the desperate hope that this was all some twisted dream.

'Don't be too hard on him,' Mark said. 'On Gareth, I mean.'

'Too hard? I'll bloody-well kill him if we get out of this alive.'

'It was me and Monkey who torched the cars. Gareth was only there for the ride a couple of times. He had nothing to do with it, I swear to God.'

'Shut up,' Angharad said, though she felt her anger at Gareth diminish. She knew he wasn't evil, just stupid. 'We'll talk about it later. For now, let me drive.'

She tightened her grip on the wheel. Confidence returned as she steered the Cavalier past the mini-roundabout and she was able to hit the accelerator again. Within seconds the world was a blur on the other side of the glass and all she could do was pray the lights at the end of the road were green, or at least that there was no-one coming the other way because she had no intention of stopping if they were red. She risked tearing her eyes away from the road long enough to peer into the mirror, and immediately wished she hadn't. The huntsman, or whatever in Christ's name it was, had not given up the chase. Indeed, if anything he had pulled ahead of the fog, the pack close behind, still obscured but only partly, as Angharad could make out the individual hounds. There were dozens of them, eyes blazing a fierce unnatural scarlet. As she watched with an equal mixture of astonishment and dread, a dog dashed out of a side street, followed swiftly by another, and a third. A cat lunged after them, bounding across the road with astounding speed. Tendrils of mist snaked out from the fog bank as they neared it, curling around them until they too were masked by the seething grey. This was wrong, she told herself. Completely wrong. It wasn't some nutter with a load of dogs. It was seriously, impossibly weird. Angharad forced herself to look away from the mirror and the uncanny scene it framed. She had to concentrate even more now that she understood the magnitude of the threat against them. The only thing that mattered was getting away. The traffic lights were visible in the distance, at the bottom of Sketty Lane where it met Oystermouth Road at a right-angle, blazing as red as the hellish eyes of the hounds. Green, green, green, Angharad found herself thinking, in the ridiculous belief she could change them through force of will alone. But they wouldn't change. Of course they wouldn't, she chided herself, easing off the gas in the hope the lights would trip through amber to green before the Cavalier was on top of them. Above the growl of the engine she heared a harsh sound lacerate the night; the unmistakable sound of hounds baying.

'Step on it,' Gareth screamed. 'They're gaining on us.'

As she rammed her foot down again she glanced in the wing mirror, panicking when she saw how close they were before she remembered the magnifying effect. The pack was huge and growing with each passing second. Small shapes shot out of gardens and the forest of shadows that was Singleton Park, to be swallowed up by the mist, which welcomed them like old friends. Something white swooped out of the sky in front of the car. Angharad screamed as it smacked into the windscreen with a sickening crunch before tumbling onto the bonnet and spinning off into the darkness, leaving behind a clump of broken feathers glued to the starred glass by a thick stain of red. Before Angharad had even begun to recover from the shock that had jolted through her, a dog the height of a small child barrelled across the road from their left, striking the front nearside with the sound like a cannon going off. Others joined it, as if a primal call had roused them from their slumber to join some wildlife kamikaze cause. Creature after doomed creature hurled itself in front the Cavalier only to bounce off the metal as ineffectually as hail. They died in silence, the only sounds a human gasp or yell from those inside the car each time the wheels bumped over yet another small corpse. The tyres began to slip in the gore, which was far more treacherous than the snow had proved. Angharad was so busy concentrating on steering out of skids she failed to register the traffic lights bearing down on them until Mark's hoarse yell made her look straight ahead.

'Left, left, left,' he screamed but Angharad spun the wheel too late and instead of turning into Oystermouth Road the Cavalier screeched into the car park on the opposite side of the junction. Gravity and inertia worked their malevolent magic and the car began to tilt over on the driver's side. Tyres shrieked their soprano protests. The pressure on the damaged windscreen intensified until it imploded with a deafening crack. Without thinking, Angharad clamped her eyes shut, instinctively raising one hand to protect them. Glass stung the flesh like a thousand tiny wasps but she barely noticed in the whirl of confusion. Then Mark's body slammed into hers, their heads cracking with sufficient force to fill her sight with an explosion of whiteness. From behind she heard Gareth grunt and guessed he must have been hurled against the door. There was a sudden loud thump and the Cavalier flipped on its side, metal screeching against concrete as it spun along the ground. A towering darkness raced out of the night to meet it and the car came to a bone-crunching halt. Every nerve in Angharad's body cried out as the seat-belt did its work. At that point she blacked out, entering a state of blessed non-existence that her battered flesh willingly embraced.

It was a short-lived respite. Before she had fully gained consciousness, Angharad was aware of pressure on her arms and the feel of concrete scraping the skin on her back. She blinked away confusion until her mind had sorted out the jigsaw puzzle of sensations that assaulted her dazed senses. Memories of the crash came back to her, though only as if she had read about it or seen it in a film rather than experienced it herself. That vicariousness acted as a cushion, placing her one step removed from brutal reality, just as it shielded her from the agony in her limbs and the fierce sensation of heat all around.

'What – ?' she gasped. She managed to raise her head, unable to suppress a gasp of pain as she did, and saw the upturned Cavalier was on fire. Beyond it, a burning river flowed from its ruptured fuel tank towards the road. She looked forward again and could see Mark, gripping her ankles with both hands and pulling her away from the conflagration. The skin on his face seemed to melt and flow, a trick of the firelight compounded by shadow and the dark flow of blood that cascaded from the rent in his forehead. He was crying. Tears carved glistening parallel lines down his cheeks. 'Mark, stop,'

Angharad said, feeling some of her strength return.

He shook his head violently. 'It's my fault. He's fucking dead because of me.'

Angharad felt his grip on her ankles slacken. She pulled her feet free then curled them underneath her, pushing on the ground with one hand and steadying herself with the other as she eased herself upright. Her head spun alarmingly and she almost fell, but the giddy spell was over in seconds. 'What?' she said in confusion. 'Who's dead?'

Mark did not respond. He did not need to. The stench of smoke and the crackle of flame was answer enough. 'Gareth,' she said, the name little more than an agonising choke in her throat. Her legs felt weak again and she sank back to the ground. Shudders made her body convulse. No, she thought helplessly. It can't be. Not Gareth. But when she looked at the car she knew it had to be true. Nothing could have survived that. The roaring, petrol-fuelled flames had even started to engulf the bottle bank the Cavalier had crashed into. Gareth was gone. She could not take it in. Her brain had gone instantly numb, protecting her from the onslaught of grief she knew she should have felt. Instead she was speared by guilt as flashes of their rows and the times she'd hated him because of the way he'd treated her leapt into her mind. Now she would gladly have him treat her like shit, if that's what it took to bring him back. 'Gareth,' she said again, feeling a hollowness in her chest that threatened to spread through her body with the same speed and ferocity as the fire that had become her brother's funeral pyre. She was vaguely aware of Mark's arms encircling her, holding her close. Then he went suddenly rigid.

Angharad tried to blink away tears of pain and loss in order to see whatever it was that had startled him. Her vision was so misty she could make out nothing. Then fright tugged at her heart with icy fingers with the dawning realisation that there was nothing wrong with her sight. The flames were dimmer now, shrouded by the rolling fog which had swept across the car park to engulf her and Mark while they were too busy suffering to notice. The baying that had pursued them down Sketty Lane had ceased and the creatures and the hunter who led them made no sound as they approached. The murkiness turned the outside world into a ghost of its former self. Lethargy crept over and through Angharad like an infection carried on the vaporous air. It no longer bothered her that Gareth was dead and that the two of them would soon be dead too. Even the sight of the pack slowly advancing, the huntsman rising above them, failed to rouse her. She was a rabbit snared in the lights of an onrushing vehicle, so mystified by the sight that it never even thought of running away while it still could. Then a sharp pain speared through her befuddled brain and she blinked and stared around in confusion. Mark was staring down at her, eyes hooded as if he was drunk.

'S-sorry I had to do that,' he said with an exaggerated shrug, sounding well and truly smashed.

'Do what?' Angharad realised she too sounded pissed.

'Hit you,' he said. He nodded towards the pack, which had halted maybe thirty yards away from them. 'Fucking things did something to us. I wanted to sleep.'

'Me too.' She was still terribly drowsy and fought against it with every ounce of strength she could summon, realising with a jolt of surprise that she loved her life, for all its failings, too much to want to lay down and die. Without a word the two of them struggled to their feet, clinging to each other for balance when they eventually managed to stand, so badly were they swaying. All the while Angharad kept one eye on the pack, expecting them to leap forward at any moment. But they remained utterly motionless, as if waiting for a signal whose nature she could not comprehend. Maybe they won't attack us if we keep still, she thought desperately. Maybe they only want the chase.

At that moment, almost as if he read her mind, the huntsman stepped forward, a shadow giant whose impenetrable darkness was troubled neither by the street lamps nor the flames that boiled into the night. A low rumbling arose from the hounds behind him, and Angharad knew with absolute certainty that the moment had come. Time to die.

'Move,' Mark hissed, putting a hand in the small of her back and shoving her away. 'Make a run for the beach. I'll go the other way, lead them away from you.'

'No way,' she said. 'If we go, we go together.'

Mark's mouth was a thin line of determination. 'We'll both die together. Gareth's already dead because of me. I don't want you killed as well. Now get going!'

And before Angharad could offer any further protest, he was gone, tearing across the car park towards Oystermouth Road at an angle that took him away from the dogs and their master. The pack responded with uncanny speed, bursting into sudden motion, closing the gap between themselves and their quarry in a matter of seconds. A scream rose in Angharad's throat as she saw Mark stumble and fall. His screams drowned it out. The beasts swarmed over him, fog circling them like a spectator. Angharad caught a brief glimpse of Mark's outstretched arm, mauled hand spraying blood. One of the beasts scuttled away, something long and pale gripped in its mouth. It cast a baleful glance Angharad's way before rejoining the pack. Needed no further prompting, she began to run towards the beach simply because it was where Mark had told her to go. Maybe he'd thought the tide was in and she could swim to safety. Angharad didn't care, not as long as she could find some way of getting out of there. Away from the nightmare.

Snow on the grass bank threatened to undo her and she almost cried with relief when she hit the foreshore path, which was as clear as the roads had been. Without hesitation she jumped from the low wall at the other side and plunged the short distance to the beach. She fell when she landed but only onto soft sand. Although the force of impact was enough to wind her at least it did not add to the injuries she had sustained in the crash, which had started to howl with every move she made. Could be worse, she told herself, angry at her self-centeredness. I could be Gareth, or Mark.

The lights of Oystermouth Road did not penetrate this far into the darkness. Neither did the glow from the blazing car. Whether the pack's supernatural powers had anything to do with that, Angharad had no way of knowing. All she did know was that she was blind and the fall had left her with no idea as to which direction she faced. She listened as hard as she could for the sound of surf but all she could hear was the slow whistle of a sea breeze and the distant crackle of the fire. With no other option to choose from she began to move forwards, bent over slightly, hands held out before her. She had not travelled far when her foot struck something which sent her sprawling. Angharad rolled over quickly and pushed herself to her feet, wiping and spitting sand from her mouth.

Whatever it was she had tripped over had felt too soft to be a rock. A drunk, maybe, sleeping it off. If so, she did not want to be around when he woke. Angharad had started to move away when an orange glow from the direction of the car park suddenly lit up the beach around her. The fire must have spread, she thought, its heat drying out and devouring the surrounding grass. As dim as it was, the light revealed she had not been walking away from the sea wall as she'd thought, but simply parallel to it. The path was a mere matter of yards away from where her. On it, staring down at her with a bared-teeth look of blatant hunger, stood the dogs. Mist rolled over them as if imitating the breaking of the distant waves. The hunter had maintained his position slightly to the fore of the pack, a shadow so dark it made a mockery of the surrounding night.

Angharad looked around wildly, seeking a means of escape but as far as she could tell there was no way out. Then she happened to glance down and, in the soft flickering light, saw that what she had stumbled over was her father's body. There was no slow dawning realisation; as soon as she cast eyes on him, she knew. His coat and his grey-black hair were instantly recognisable, as were those scuffed leather cowboy boots he wore whenever he went out, like they were some kind of talisman. But they had not protected him from harm, not this time. His arms were flung open wide, fingers missing. Most of his face had gone, too. The sand around him was stained black, and spread out in such a way that suggested he had been hurled from the path to the beach.

Angharad's mind whirled. She felt faint. A sob escaped her throat, a single harsh bark. Until the moment she found him dead she had not understood, she still loved the old man whose body she now cradled in trembling arms. For all his failings, his drunkenness and his hung-over rages, he was still her father. Now he was dead, just like Gareth and Mark. She struggled to cope with the enormity of it. Only a few hours ago she'd had all three of them. But here she was, alone. Utterly, terrifyingly alone. Angharad faced the huntsman, feeling an enormous rage boil up within her. She wanted to scream at it, run up to it and hit it with every ounce of sense she possessed. But before she could move tiny pinpricks of brilliant green appeared in the obsidian circle that Angharad assumed was its head, spiralling like miniature galaxies before coalescing into two circles of verdant light. It had eyes, Angharad realised, eyes that met hers before she could look away, rooting her to the spot.

'Who are you?' she demanded in a voice lacking venom, the huntsman's gaze having leeched her anger away. All that she wanted now was an explanation. Questions formed in her mind. As she stared into the green eyes before her, she had her answer. It was impossible, yet she instinctively knew it to be true. Angharad had summoned the pack herself. It was she who had somehow blown the horn that roused them from whatever hellish domain they came. She even knew the moment it had happened; when she'd sat in the snow, clutching her injured hand and desperately wishing for freedom, for a way out of her lousy, limited life. Yes, she had loved Gareth and Mark, her father as well. But at the same time they had unwittingly condemned her to an existence she hated. No longer, though. Now she had her freedom, even if she could never accept what she'd paid for it.

The huntsman's green gaze held hers momentarily, then it turned and vanished into the mist, the pack following as swiftly and silently as will o' the wisps.

The firelight began to die. Beyond the sea, the night sky started to lighten, a harbinger of dawn. In the distance Angharad heard sirens. She could stay here and try to explain what had happened to the police, or she could take the chance offered to her and start her life anew. Leaving now would seem like a betrayal of those she had loved. Yet staying would not bring them back. Crying softly, Angharad lowered her father's head gently to the sand, then stood and made her way on unsteady legs to the path.

CURVES AND SHARP EDGES

Tim Lebbon

After the ruin there was a place called Dena, ruled over by the tyrannical Mahje. It was full of wonders and awash with stories from afar, and in this land dogs could fly and sheep could talk. But these were mundane things to the people of Dena; the real magic dwelled within the imaginations of those who lived there.

Stern had made a business out of helping people access this magic. He sold them oils that let them drift away to extraordinary lands, at least in their minds. The oils were marketed as being from distant, unknown places, but Stern actually distilled them in the shed behind his house from plant extracts and the crushed shells of tortoises. Both were free, and the tortoise meat went some way to feeding his wife and daughter in the more difficult times.

And lean times were frequent in Dena. Lean times like now. Stern's wife Katrina was the shadow of her former voluptuous self, an echo of the rounded woman he had married twenty years before. All their good food went to their daughter Suze, and they were often left with the gristle from between two bones, the core of an old apple. Stern's oils were good and sought-after, but these days the main wealth of the village was possessed by the Mahje, and the rest went hungry. Stern's oils could be afforded by fewer and fewer people.

For the first time in his life, Stern owed money. Grim, the village banker, had lent him a hundred dreds, and with the extortionate interest he chose to charge, Stern was now three hundred dreds in the red. Katrina did not know. Suze was unaware of such stressful matters. Stern carried the weight of his family on his shoulders. Ironically, the more their combined weight slithered away into hunger, the greater the stress on Stern.

He passed a flock of babbling sheep on what he hoped would be his last trip to see Grim. 'Barmy grasses,' they wittered, 'crazy crops, gooish grazing, see the height of dead grasses.' Not for the first time, Stern wondered at a god who gave such senseless creatures the power of speech. The last person who had held a coherent conversation with a sheep was March the Miner, and now he was supposedly adrift on the Specific Sea, seeking his fortune on the far-off shores.

Stern came to Grim's home, an ostentatious affair that reached for the sky, not quite getting there before the various spires and turrets were topped by expensive ornamentation. He wished once again that such a rich man would forget a measly debt of three hundred dreds; but his richness came from never forgetting. Stern would have to argue, negotiate, and plead if necessary. He would not stand and watch his family dying before his helpless eyes.

'Mr Grim, Sir, I beseech you,' he began, but already Grim had turned and pushed his front door shut. Stern stuck his foot in the door. 'Hear me out, Mr Grim. I insist you hear me out.'

Grim turned, eyebrows raised in mock surprise. Everything was a sham with Grim. After thirty years lending money, he had seen and heard almost everything, and very little shocked him. 'Insist, do you, Stern? Well, and does your once-beautiful wife Katrina open her legs when you 'insist' with her, eh? Does she bend over the stove and let you rut as she cooks, eh? Eh?'

'My relations with my wife are none of your business, Mr Grim–'

'Oh, but they are, Stern. Because, you see, if you do not pay up the four hundred dreds – did I tell you you've passed another interest period? – within the day, then your family will be very much my business. I shall own them, Stern, and that rancid little house of yours. Including your stinking little shed where you make oils for the masses.'

'The oils are imported–'

'Sheep piss! I know everything, Stern. It's my job to investigate my future holdings. Your daughter, I think, fattened in my cellar and groomed and trained by my slaves, would fetch an acceptable price on the whoreships.'

Stern felt like crying, but knew that a man such as Grim would not countenance such behaviour on the doorstep of his home. Tears were for the defeated, anyway, and Stern would not – could not – give in so easily. 'Mr Grim, Sir, I implore you. I have a hundred dreds here, in my hand. That is what I borrowed from you, that is what I return. As and when I can afford it, I will hand you more money for interest. But my family starves. Out of all of us, only my dear daughter Suze had eaten meat in the last ten days. My wife and I survive on potatoes and windfalls from the village deadfruit tree. And that, as you know, is more bad than good.'

'Deadfruit is food, if you are reduced to those levels.' Grim made a great show of calling a slave and tearing the leg from a roast chicken she brought on a silver platter. He bit into it before he spoke again, so that he sprayed chewed meat over Stern. 'But a hundred is not enough. I will have it, surely. But for your impertinence, it will merely pay the fine I would otherwise impose on you for visiting me without an appointment.'

Stern closed his eyes, unable to prevent the juices from flowing in his mouth. The smell of the chicken was almost enough to drive him to violence, so he turned and left. Attacking Grim would do nothing to help Katrina and Suze.

'The hundred, Stern?'

Stern considered running, but he knew he would not get far in his weakened state. Slaves though they were, Grim's attendants were still better fed than many of the common villagers. They would overtake him within a dozen paces, beat him, steal his money and perhaps leave him with a knife in his guts for his pains. The Mahje would turn a blind eye, as Grim was his banker. Only his family would mourn his dusty, pointless death.

Stern turned, opened his eyes. 'Here's your money, Grim. Your blood money. I hope the death of my child, when it comes, sits heavily on your bloated conscience.' He threw the bag of coins at Grim's fat feet.

Grim smiled. Chicken skin hung between his teeth, grease dribbled down his chin and became lost in the clotted beard which hung there. 'I have no conscience, Stern,' he said. 'And the death of your child would only make it easier for you to pay me back. May God grant it soon.'

Stern turned and hurried away as fast as he could without tripping and losing what little dignity he still retained. Behind him Grim burped, farted, laughed. As Stern entered the outskirts of the festering village once more, his anger was overtaken by a mortal, deadening sense of failure.

The decision he took was fuelled by hunger, fear and dread. He saw everything falling apart around him, and he did not wish to be there to see it end. Stern loved his wife and daughter dearly, but when he left them, he was thinking only of himself. His oils helped, but the initial intention was there, burning within him, an eternal guilt.

He had only ever been into the woods to gather secret handfuls of plants and roots for his oils, and then only into the outskirts. He knew that they were said to stretch for a hundred miles, a distance he thought would dim his memory, perhaps, go some way to cleansing his soul.

Stern had been taking his own oils. He was disorientated, dreamy, plunging headlong through the brush with nary a thought for his family. Even now Katrina would be panicking, calling weakly out through the door where she expected him to return within the hour. His daughter would be huddled in the corner, waiting for food and milk, too sick to move when she dirtied herself. And his wife, too wretched to clean her up.

But Stern saw only the woods parting before him, heard the secret rustlings of unknown animals, the conspiratorial song of birds passing messages through the treetops. He paused briefly in his flight, undid a phial, spread more oil on his upper lip. It was the oil of forgetfulness, though he was now unsure of this truth, and he had forgotten why he was taking it.

By lunchtime, he had traveled six miles into the woods. The trees had changed from the familiar tall, pert growths at the fringes to gnarled old monsters from thousands of years before. These trees had seen much: the ruin; the plague of wraiths that swept through humanity centuries ago; the unwary wanderer, lost and forgotten in the woods. Stern tried to keep as far away from the trees as he could – their trunks were twisted into malicious grins, their branches held spiked pain for the casual traveler. But the further he went, the closer together they grew, as if time were allowing them an eventual, eternal union.

The clearing surprised and frightened him as much as the trees. By the time he was at the centre of the open space the oil had done its job, and the monstrous trees had slipped his mind. The sun beat down with a vengeance, making up for lost time. Tall grasses waved slowly in tune with the breeze. In the centre of the clearing stood a huge, beautiful tree, taller than any Stern had ever seen, its bark older and more pitted than the surface of the moon, branches heavy with lush foliage. But whereas the trees in the forest held a sense of menace behind their aged bark, this one exuded an aura of welcome, calmness and serenity.

Immediately, the effect of Stern's oil vanished. He stumbled slightly as he recalled his journey through the forest, glanced back where the darkness began at the edge of the clearing, half expecting to see branches and roots inching slowly towards him. He remembered Katrina and Suze. How they relied upon him. How Suze was becoming weaker and more poorly even though she did eat all the meat they managed to buy or catch. Tears smudged his vision and he let them come, content that he was alone in this strange place, happy that here he could purge his anguish without the threat of being seen. It would not do for a man to cry. But here, in the presence of this ancient tree perhaps as old as time itself, Stern felt that crying marked him as a real man. He wished that Katrina were here to see him.

He approached the tree and walked around its huge trunk. It took him nearly a hundred steps to circle it, and by the time he arrived at his starting point he felt a weariness washing through him. In his shoulder-bag he had some hunks of stale bread and a horn of rancid wine, as well as a pick and mix collection of his oils. He brought the oils out first. The oil of forgetfulness was almost half empty, and he discarded it without another thought. He did not wish to forget. He wanted to overcome. Next he found the oil of lust, and he felt a stirring in his loins simply remembering what this could do. He dropped it back into the bag, along with the other phials. For now, food would suffice. Then, after he had rested, he would return to his wife and daughter. He would take no oils for the journey – he wanted to experience each fear, every emotion, feel them line his mind like a shield of experience against the tenacious Grim. If he could defeat the forest, pass out from it alive, then that fat old banker was surely an easier foe to win over.

He ate his bad bread, though it tasted good. He drank the sharp wine, let his eyelids droop. As he drifted from the land of waking, he let his senses explore this strange new domain. Through partially closed eyes he could look up and see the pleasing curves of the tree branches, the gentle ovals of its millions of leaves, perhaps a leaf for every life on the planet. Songs from the forest held no sharp edges, only the calming curves of happiness and a basic joy with nature that man had ignored for far too long. The smells of the area were gentle, benevolent, inspiring memories of far better times in the past though, occasionally, they seemed to be some other past than that experienced by Stern. When he opened his mouth, he could almost taste the softness of the place on the breeze, a hint of mint – perhaps this is what solitude really tasted like.

His eyelids closed. At some point he drifted off to sleep, passing that mysterious threshold which has concerned philosophers and thinkers for so long.

He woke. Something struck him on the cheek, something with a sharp edge that parted his skin like a knife. Stern opened his eyes and saw that the sky had cracked apart into a million irregular, angry pieces. It stood frozen above him, ready at any moment to tumble down and crush him to death. He gasped, hardly able to draw breath, but then realised that he was looking through the branches of the tree. The revelation did little to comfort him, however. The tree was bare, every leaf having died and fallen, and now the only leaf visible was that which had fallen onto his face and cut him. He stood, staggering with shock and a terror which he knew had always been there, waiting, from the moment he had entered the clearing. The place was now full of sharp edges: the accusing branches of the huge tree, pointing skyward in frozen death; sharp cries of hunting and killing from the forest; the tang of rot on the air, a decay so thick that Stern was afraid to breathe, lest he take it in and be corrupted.

He turned to run, but he was far too late. With a rumble, then a roar, the tree lifted from its ancient home in the ground and burst skyward. At first, Stern thought he would escape. He was away from the trunk, after all, and fear gave him speed. But the ground beneath him bucked and rippled, and it took only seconds for the whole clearing to erupt into an explosion of noise, flying earth, scampering and slithering creatures pulled up from below by the tree's roots. Stern grabbed a root, realising that he was already aflight and a hundred steps up into the air. To fall now would be fatal.

He looked up and back. The tree was dwarfed by its root system, which spread out in a great fan three times as far from the trunk as the loftiest branches. Set as they were against the settling sun, the branches seemed to squirm and twist, as if in umbrage at this sudden uprooting.

Stern wanted to scream, but the sight below him prevented any sound from leaving his body. He must be miles up. In the distance, Dena sat squat between two mountains, minute and irrelevant. The root he was gripping onto was slippery, like the inside of a dead animal. Or a living one. It let off a stench, cloying, acidic. With every breath, Stern felt consciousness fleeing further earthward.

He felt very small.

And eventually, even through fear, he slept.

When Stern awoke, he was in a different place.

He was where the sea met the land. If he looked one way there was only water, endless and grey and huge. In the other direction, the land rolled flat and featureless towards some indistinct horizon.

Turning a full circle, he realised an uncomfortable truth. The horizon was flat; there was no hint of a curve. The only sign of movement was the intermittent flow of the sea onto the beach, before it was driven back again in a never-ending give and take. The tree had seemingly planted itself into the beach, stretching its roots out to the water. Stern was too terrified of his new surroundings, however, to worry about the tree. He walked along the sand, searching for any tell-tale marks which may indicate life, even civilisation. But there was nothing. No enigmatic trail of bird footprints, no wormholes blowing bubbles, no shells. Nothing. Nothing alive apart from him, and the tree.

Something flashed momentarily, blinding him. He squinted into the sun and shaded his eyes, searching for whatever had sent the signal. It came again, this time from somewhere else. He moved along the beach, parallel to the line of surf. He kicked something and yelped with pain and shock. Looking down he saw a small metallic object, completely spherical, its surface a stainless silver.

He picked it up. He knew almost immediately what it was for, a knowledge that appeared like a forgotten memory recalled by a certain smell: if he placed this sphere next to the womb of a pregnant woman, it would tell whether the baby was healthy, what sex it was, what position it was in. Stern, wide-eyed and agog, dropped the sphere instantly into his shoulder-bag. It was priceless, ultimately precious, almost a God-send.

Which thought made Stern wonder just where the hell he was.

Another gleam caught his eye, a dozen steps further along the beach.

The object, when Stern picked it up, was of the same material as the first, but it was pyramidal in shape. It was very heavy, even though it was only the size of his hand. As with the first, he knew instantly what it was for: set so that the apex pointed exactly vertical, the object would predict from which direction, and at what intensity, the next bad weather front would come. The relevant side would light up – the brighter it became, the worse the storm would be.

How many lives could be saved?

He found a cube that would cure blindness. A hoop, in the shape of a halo, which when passed around the relevant limb would burn out arthritis for weeks or months at a time.

Stern was stunned, so much so that he sat on the sand and stared skyward. The mysterious knowledge he was gaining was scaring him, so he did not pick up any more objects, even though he could now see hundreds of blinking shapes scattered across the endless beach. He wondered whether they were washed up from the sea, and what strange foreign shore they had come from.

He wondered whether he would recognise the star constellations, should he still be here come night time.

It was almost as if his musing provoked the tree into action. Stern heard a roar, the hiss of sand. He stood and ran as it shivered in the ground, hauling itself from the sand, suddenly rocketing skywards once again. He caught hold of a trailing root and pulled himself up into the safety of the complex root system. He looked down for as long as he could, before the stench from the roots put him back to sleep, but still he could only make out the sea, and the beach, with the frothy white line of surf dividing them in two.

Nothing else.

Stern had to claw his way to the surface as the tree's roots re-buried themselves, but he was not afraid. It was dark when he plunged back into the woods, past the angry looking old trees, heading for the village of Dena, but he was concerned only with the shiny treasures in his shoulder bag. Because he knew he would make it back home. Fate had guided him to the tree, attached him to the trailing roots, allowed him the insight with which to see the secrets of the shining objects. Perhaps fate had even encouraged him to leave his home, pretending to abandon his wife and daughter but, in reality, heading towards salvation. The thought was pleasing, so he grasped onto it. He did not want to lose the comfort it afforded him.

Dena was in darkness. He could sense the fluttering agitation of dogs in

heat as they swooped over the rooftops. Occasionally a frustrated or trium-
phant bark would break the night, but mainly it was quiet. Even the muttering
mad sheep were silent, dreaming unknown dreams in their woolly sleep.

Stern strode confidently down the main street, unafraid, almost smug
with his new-found wealth. Grim could not refuse this. He would never turn
down such wonders, and then Stern and Katrina would be free of the debt. He
could build his life again.

Perhaps, in that strange place of land and sea, there was a creation
which transmuted desires into oils, and vice versa?

Even the stink of human shit, stagnant in overflowing drains, did not
deflect his good humour as he approached his home. A mass of flies lifted
from the mess, darkening the night even more, and it was as their secret whisper faded to quieter corners of Dena that Stern heard the noise – muffled,
anxious, a squeal of discomfort.

Katrina.

The door had never been locked or stiff, but it took Stern frantic seconds
of shoving and kicking to open it enough to gain entry into his home. A thick
coat was the reason for his struggle, sat behind the door like a dead guard
dog. Stern recognised it, even as comprehension dawned about the sounds.
The light of the room seemed darker than outside, blacker even than the
dead-of-night woods, because Grim had made it so.

Katrina was trying to hold him back. Grim – naked, sweating, obese
rolls of flab turning him into a melting marshmallow – pawed at her, seemingly relishing the scuffle. 'What's mine, is mine,' he said, again and again.
His manhood hid semi-erect between dimpled thighs. Matted hair tufted out
from between his huge white buttocks.

'What's mine, is mine.'

'No...no...no...Suze...Suze...Suze...' Katrina was crying, but the words
found their way through her distress.

'Suze?' Stern said. His daughter. What had the animal done to his
daughter?

'Daddy?' Suze was in the corner of the room, tied to a chair. Made to
watch.

'Huh?' Grim's jaw dropped in surprise and he jerked his head around.

Stern felt a rush of helplessness and dread attack him.

'What's mine, is mine,' Grim said, recovering his composure, his ap-
pearance transmuting instantly from ridiculous to intimidating as his eyes
hardened. 'You ran away, you weak shit, and now I've come to take my dues.
Leave. Your wife no longer knows you.' He turned back to Katrina, and the
look in her eyes – desperate, disbelieving, accusing – almost drove Stern to
attack Grim there and then. But an attack would inevitably only ever land

blows on himself, and they would be knife blows. Grim would shout, he would call, and however obvious the situation it was he, Stern, who would be accused. No escape route that way, nothing which could really save him there.

'Here are your dues,' Stern said. He threw the bag, both wincing and smiling as it struck the fat banker on the stomach.

Grim grunted, but the glow of avarice outshone his anger. He grabbed the bag before it could hit the floor, ignoring Katrina now that there was something else to intrigue him.

Stern nodded to his wife, finding it impossible to smile. He should have been here for her, not in the strange forest, no matter how much he believed fate had taken him there. She was shivering in the corner, holding her torn dress to her chest, her stare falling somewhere between Stern and Grim.

'What nonsense is this?' Grim growled. He had opened the bag and hauled out one of the silvery objects – the hoop – and seemed ready to throw it at Stern. 'I've no use for pretty fancies. A whore might take this, maybe, to eat your meat. But why offend me-?'

'It's something very precious,' Stern cut in, realising instantly that if Grim did not suffer from rheumatism or blindness, then he would have great trouble proving his bold statement.

Grim stepped towards him, unconcerned at his nakedness. He would be more embarrassed standing there nude in front of a dog. 'You useless drug dealer, you'd better just tell me now what you're up to, or let me take my dues. And the longer you keep me waiting –' he glanced at Suze, huddled crying in the chair '– the more dues I may decide to take.'

That flash of anger again, subdued instantly by the certainty that any aggression would end in imprisonment, at the very least. Stern closed his eyes, seeking composure. 'If you suffer from rheumatism,' he said, 'this will cure you for a time.'

'Shit.'

'It will cure you. Just... look at it.' He wished Grim could see what he had seen on that strange shore, understand as he had how this remarkable object could be put to use.

And then Grim smiled. It was a grotesque sight, because it was so unnatural. Stern would rather have seen a slug laughing that this fat pig smiling in his house. The banker stared at the hoop in his hand ... and Stern realised that he had seen what it could do.

'What else?' He asked. He took the silver shapes from the bag one by one, his eyes lighting up every time he saw something new. Eventually, he had the four objects in front of him, two in each hand.

'We may, perhaps, disregard the debt this time,' Grim said mildly.

'There will be no other loan. And there will be no word spoken of my ... kind leniency.'

Stern roared inside, but relief rushed through him. 'You are most magnificent,' he said, bowing so that he did not have to look into the man's eyes as he said it.

Grim left after hastily dressing in his finery. Stern and Katrina untied Suze and huddled close together, sharing warmth in the room that suddenly felt so cold, not speaking, just relishing their escape.

Later, Katrina asked Stern what had really been in the bag.

'Nothing,' he said.

Katrina persisted.

'Our salvation,' Stern said, but he would not be drawn on the subject any more. And when Katrina mentioned it again later that night, he feigned sleep.

Grim hobbled through the night on legs still shaking from lust. The woman had almost been his, and then the drug seller had interrupted. True, he had left the place with much more than he had arrived with – treasures and devices beyond the dreams of mere human avarice – but still his ardour thumped in his trousers, demanding release. Later, he promised himself, the women of his house would be rudely awakened.

But not yet. Now, he had something to show the Mahje. He knew that the Mahje was a useful ally, and though the old chieftain had said many times how Grim was his friend, where greed was involved friendships were relegated to childish memories. Grim was only too aware of how angry the Mahje would be if he discovered what Grim was hiding, so the only recourse was to submit the devices to the great leader immediately, and in the process ... Well, there was still the mayorship of Dena to consider.

So thinking, Grim made his way through the secret dark. Not even the sheep were chattering tonight. Perhaps they could sense a tension in the air.

'And you are trying to tell me,' said the Mahje, 'that a mere drug seller – an oil man, for pity's sake – gave you these ... things.' He called them 'things', but his eyes labelled them wonders. He coveted the devices as he spoke, touching them, caressing them as he would the smooth globe of a woman's breast.

'An oil seller I tell you, Majesty. A simple man, a splatter of dog shit who owed me three hundred dreds.' Grim was sitting cross-legged, as was the custom when addressing the Mahje, and his feet were beginning to go to sleep. He shifted occasionally, but every time he lifted his weight even slightly, the Mahje's guards tensed and the rattle of ready battle-armour whispered around the great hall.

'And this oil man ... this drug man ... his name is ...?'

'Stern, Majesty.'

'Stern.' The Mahje did not speak for a long while. He sat back on his humming-bird bone throne, gently tapping his fingers, humming softly as if mocking the dead source of his seat. 'Why, do you think, unpleasant Grim, that this Stern gave you only four items?'

'Majesty?' Grim frowned, but already he knew what the Mahje was saying. He had been foolish in his greed, eager to leave with the four items of wonder when there were, inevitably, many more waiting to be taken from wherever Stern had found these.

'Bring this Stern,' the Mahje said. 'I wish to see him.'

Grim stood, his feet relieved that the audience was over. He bowed and shuffled backwards from the throne room, wincing in agony as pins and needles pricked the flesh of his feet and ankles. As the great doors were closed behind him he slowly stood to his full, rounded height, trying not to gasp as the circulation returned to his lower extremities. The guard stared at him with a face so devoid of expression that Grim thought perhaps he was dead, and the Mahje had resurrected him for the boring duty he now took.

Perhaps, in this strange place where the oil seller had found his useful toys, there was a device which did just that.

'You can't go again,' Katrina whimpered, though her voice wailed in Stern's ears. 'You can't leave me ... please, don't leave me. What if ...' She trailed off, but her quick glance in Grim's direction finished what she could not say.

'He's coming as well,' Stern replied. He felt hopeless. He hugged his wife to him and heard a derisory snort from the fat banker behind him, but he was as helpless as a dog without wings. There was nothing he could do, no way he could ignore the instruction of the Mahje without being arrested and, probably, prosecuted for disobeying an order from His Majesty. And so – a goat on a leash, a mouse against the Mahje's lion and the banker's cat – Stern knew he had no choice.

'But you may never come back. What then? How will Suze and I survive then, a family without you to provide? Perhaps the new Mahje may be kind enough to take Suze into his brothel, but me? What about me? Who will want my tired, dry body?' Katrina was crying, but they were hot tears of anger as well as sobs of sadness, burning across her reddening cheeks, almost steaming.

Stern had never heard his wife talk like this before. He knew that she understood the real way of things, but in their own little way they had managed to brush aside some of the uneven trappings of modern life. Stern was the main provider, true, but he was also the cooker and the cleaner of Suze's nappies when she was younger. Behind closed doors, of course. In public, he had to be a man.

Grim snorted again – a guttural sound which presumably passed for a laugh from this humourless monster – and this time Stern could not help himself. He spun around, fists clenching at his sides, his wife's hands biting into his biceps as she felt them stiffening in anger. Somehow reason overcame the acid desire he had to kill Grim there, grind his face into the uneven, dusty floor of their home. Instead, he threw the banker a glare that under normal circumstances, he knew he would be whipped for.

Grim's face fell in disbelief, but then he stepped back. For an instant the three of them remained like that – Stern staring at the malodorous banker, Katrina ready to hold her husband back, Grim white-faced and offended – before the fat man turned and left.

'Oh glory,' Katrina said, and burst into tears. 'What will become of us?'

Stern hugged his wife to him, trying to give her strength as she had done for him so many times throughout their life together. There was a terrible finality about things, as if fate were guiding their words with the power of prior knowledge.

'Love, I must leave now. But think of me every second. Always remember me, whether I return or not. If you love me forever, it will help, because love is magic.'

Katrina could not bring herself to reply until Stern had walked away with the other two men. 'I love you,' she eventually managed to whisper, but if he did answer then the sound of his voice was swallowed by a loud, phlegmy cough from Grim.

Stern held some vague hope that the tree he had found was a good tree, and that it would avoid giving itself away to the like of Grim and the corrupted Mahje. But geography allowed no favouritism, at least to the insignificant world of humans, and they soon found themselves standing under the great tree in the wide clearing in the woods. Grim and the Mahje were impatient for the magic to happen, and Stern continued to assure them that it would, even though he felt doubt tug at him.

Had he really come here, sat down and been transferred to some alien shore? Did he truly believe that Nature would open the door for him again, after he had used the gifts for such a shallow cause as paying a debt?

I will be rich, thought the Mahje. Rich enough to buy a dozen cities. Governor, soon. And then? King? Oh, King, and then I shall know the true meaning...

I will be powerful, thought Grim. Beyond the power of mere money, of which I have mountains. Power in the minds of men, power to give and to take at my own whim...

I will no longer be hungry, thought Stern. Katrina and Suze will grow healthy, and my wife and I will grow old happy, content, if not rich. For who would see a mere oil seller rise in the ranks of the city? And would I want to? But food, drink, clothes...

So thinking, the three men fell asleep beneath the tree.

And awoke to find the ground in turmoil.

On the horizon, infinity.

Grim gasped at the sight, and for once his buffish posture slumped as pure emotion swept through him. Stern, who had seen it before, found it all the more stunning for that. The sea – a seemingly never-ending tumult of white-tipped waves, coming from nowhere – went on forever, striving to reach the sky at some distant, barely seen conjunction of reality and imagination.

And beneath their feet, the tree burrowed itself into the sand of the beach.

'Look!' said the Mahje, climbing clumsily from the tangled roots. All regality had vanished in his greedy rush to be the first to grasp what he had seen. It was a small, round object, sitting on the hot sand like a child's forgotten memory. He picked it up and gasped, a sound clawing from his throat and emerging as a rasping, pained yelp.

'Majesty, what is it?' Grim shouted, his sycophantic side re-asserting itself once more.

'I feel so many futures,' the ruler said, a smile struggling to look at home on his face. 'So much potential ... I have seed. My seed is good, at last! I can have children!'

'Majesty,' Grim said, 'I did not know you were...'

The Mahje shook his head, dismissive of the banker and the sea, ignoring even the huge tree that still shook occasionally behind them. 'Children ... successors ...' He muttered, sinking to his knees in the sand.

Stern moved slowly to one side, but his stealth was unnecessary. Already Grim was off on his own, darting hither and thither, picking up whatever shining devices he could find, various exhalations of surprise, mirth or disbelief providing an audio map of his travels. Stern wanted to sit and shove greed to one side, but human nature defeated him.

A glimmer in the sand caught his eye. Surely, more than the sun glinting from metal? This was winking at him and only him, a secretive wonder for his hands only. And it looked so beautiful and abandoned, sitting there in the sand, half buried by whatever occasional winds swept across this endless landscape.

He glanced around. In a distance much distorted by the absence of horizon, Grim and the Mahje were foraging separately for their own personal treasures. Neither of them had seen this one. This one was for him, and him alone.

Stern lifted the object from the sand. It was much heavier than it looked, and as he raised it to eye level his arms shook with the strain.

At first, he could see little that surprised him. In the highly polished surface there was Grim and the Mahje, bathed in the constant sun. Then he realised that it was not simply a reflection. The perspective was all wrong, not matching the reality of the scene ... and his own face was not there! In the image the two men were sitting, not standing. And their clothes hung on thin shoulders; their skin drooped in drapes from dried, withered flesh.

Their empty eye sockets stared indefinitely at the infinite horizon.

And there was no tree.

Stern gasped. The future, he was seeing the future, that was all this could be! But how far into the future? He glanced at the tree and saw slow movement in its roots, a steady uncovering of the vast arms as it raised itself out of the sand. Its branches quivered, shed leaves drifted down to land on the sand and water.

He looked to the Mahje and Grim, and saw that they were still dashing here and there across the sands. They had not noticed the tree's movements. He should warn them. He should call to them and point out what was happening, save their wretched souls, and perhaps if he did that then their treatment of him would–

But he had already seen what would happen to them. The bleached bones. The empty eye sockets. The jaws open in everlasting screams.

Stern felt the urge to search some more, find new miracles half-buried in the sand, keep them to himself ... but survival was a greater instinct, especially when his family's love called to him across whatever strange distances lay between them. So he hugged the device to his chest and ran.

As he did so – as if at the exact instant that its subterfuge was realised – the tree began to shake more violently, and he only just hooked one arm over a slimy root before it rocketed skywards, throwing down tons of sand in a stinging rain below it.

He looked below him at the two men, already shrinking as the tree rose and rose.

'Come back!' commanded the Mahje.

'Bastard!' shouted Grim.

'Katrina ... Suze.' thought Stern. He was a murderer now, he guessed, a killer by default. He hoped he had served his family well.

*

Four moons later, the loss of the Mahje had been almost forgotten. The village had a new ruler, as mean in many ways as the old Mahje, and the villagers had little time for reminiscing.

A new banker, too: Dour, nephew of Grim. He had raised yearly interest rates on loans by six hundred percent, and had been empowered with the right to judge and execute those who slipped behind with their payments. He was getting fat on his profits, as were his pet alligators.

Stern had crept back quietly in the night. The naked greed of the two men he had left behind meant that they had told no one of where they were going, and so Stern was never implicated in their disappearance. He had laid low for a few days nonetheless, feigning sickness as he recovered from his final trip through the forest, staring at that single object he had brought back with him. Sometimes it showed him things he knew he wanted to see. Other times he saw less savoury scenes, but they never concerned him or his family, and it was always knowledge he could use against those involved, if the need ever arose.

Mostly, it showed him the mood of the people days from now, their needs, their desires and their aims. And from that he knew which oils to blend, and what ingredients to use to make the perfect recipe.

Now there was food on the table, clothes in Suze's wardrobe and good shoes on her feet. Stern would never be a rich man, but he was far from greedy: he had his family and that was enough. Wealth to him was love, and love was magic. And real magic truly dwelled in the imagination.

CONTRIBUTORS

Derek M Fox
The author of the novels, *Recluse* and *Demon*, as well as the Enigmatic Variations collection *Treading On The Past*, Derek has just signed contracts for a book about Lord Byron. He teaches and regularly gives talks about writing. His stories probe the classical style, dwelling in the modern day, to view it with traditional values. This story is just such an example.

Steve Savile
This fine story appeared in the 1999 Enigmatic Variations collection *Icarus Descending* and was well received, earning nominations in the Stoker's and the BFS Awards lists, and an Honourable Mention is anticipated. Steve lives in Sweden, where he teaches, and writes stories of emotional depth and technical imagination. Author of the novels *The Secret Life Of Colours* and *Laughing Boy's Shadow*, as well as the e-serial *The Sufferer's Song*.

Paul Finch
A former policeman and journalist Paul now writes full time, selling anarchic cartoon scripts and TV scripts. Married to Cathy and father to Eleanor and Harry. Numerous short story sales have helped build a reputation for solid story telling and imaginative narrative drive. He is working on a novel, and has just seen his *The Shadows Beneath* collection published by Enigmatic Variations, following the success of 1999's *The Dark Satanic*. This story uses a historical background to tell a fantastic tale.

Paul Lewis
Paul has co-edited, with Steve Lockley, the *Cold Cuts* series of anthologies, as well as having numerous stories published in both the adult and young adult markets. He has also written hundreds of comedy sketches for TV and radio, sitcom pilots for BBC Wales and S4C. His first novel, with Steve Lockley, *The Ragchild* is scheduled from Razorblade Press this year.

Steve Lockley
Co-editor, with Paul Lewis, of *Cold Cuts*, and co-writer, with Paul, of his first novel, *The Ragchild*, due out from Razorblade Press this year. Steve has

had numerous stories published, and with Mike O'Driscoll was awarded a BFS Special Award for the horror convention *Welcome To My* Nightmare. This excellent story uses modern people and shows what happens to them

Tim Lebbon

His first novel *Mesmer* in 1997 was short listed for a BFS Award for Best Novel. His second novel, *Faith In The Flesh* is out now from Razorblade Press. Tim has had numerous stories published in magazines and anthologies and is currently working on his next novel. He writes stories that challenge the conventional imaginative processes, giving tangents from which to draw conclusions that are thought provoking. His novella *White* is included in the upcoming Year's Best Fantasy and Horror and Best New Horror, and his novella *Naming Of Parts* has been accepted by PS Publishing.

Bob Covington

An artist of acclaim and talent, Bob was BFS Best Cover Artist in 1999. He has produced work of variety and quality for this book and his work helps raise the overall standards.

David Bezzina

David has also produced quality work for this book and the depth of his illustrations have aided the dramatic impact of the prose. He is a talented artist.

Maynard & Sims

Have been described as "a two headed beast" which is more complimentary than most comments about us. Authors of the hardback collections *Shadows At Midnight* (1979 and 1999) and *Echoes Of Darkness* (2000) they have completed their latest adult collection, a young adult collection and a young adult novel, and are currently working on an adult novel and young adult crime novel. They have had numerous story sales including crime and young adult under different pseudonyms. They write a column and book reviews for *At The Worlds End*.

David J Howe

Commissioning editor of BFS Publications, key BFS member and organiser, keeper of Howe's Who at www.howeswho.co.uk, writer of many things including Doctor Who articles and books, reviewer, and Virgo, David had the conceptual idea and the drive for this project and we all hope it will be a success now and in the planned annual publications.

BOOKS THAT BITE

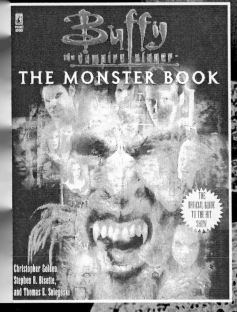

THE MONSTER BOOK

Christopher Golden,
Stephen R. Bisette,
and Thomas E. Sniegoski

Sunnydale's sexiest vampire couple revisit their English roots and embark on a riotous killing spree across war-torn 1940s Europe. Working from a known list of female Slayers-in-waiting – the "pretty maids all in a row" – Spike and Dru joyously enter into blood-frenzied slaughter.
Out November £12.99 Hardback

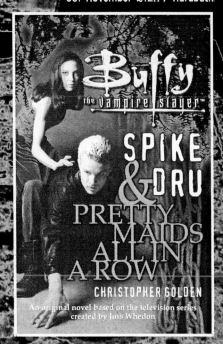

Every single monster from four seasons of the show – their origins, their background, their makeup – PLUS chapters on demons, vampires, magic users, ghosts, bogeymen, primals and the walking dead in myth, history, literature, and film. A monster book in every sense, this 370-page guide is THE essential reference for Buffy fans and all lovers of the dark and demonic.
Out Now £10.99 Paperback

POCKET BOOKS

Http://www.herebedragons.co.uk/bfs/

The British Fantasy Society publishes fantasy and dark fantasy fiction, speculative articles, artwork, reviews, interviews, comment and much more. They also organise the annual FantasyCon convention to which publishers, editors, authors and fans flock to hear the announcement of the coveted British Fantasy Awards, voted on by the members.

Membership of the BFS is open to everyone. The annual UK subscription is £20.00 which covers the acclaimed bi-monthly Newsletter and the additional BFS books and anthologies. To join, send moneys payable to the BFS together with your name and address to:

The BFS Secretary,
c/o 201 Reddish Road,
South Reddish
Stockport
SK5 7HR

Overseas membership, please write or email for current details.
The BFS reserves the right to raise membership fees.
Should the fee change, applicants for membership will be advised.

Email: syrinx.2112@btinternet.com

F20